The Bourgeois Anarchist

a novella by

Sam Gridley

Finishing Line Press
Georgetown, Kentucky

The Bourgeois Anarchist

Publisher: Leah Huete de Maines

Editor: Christen Kincaid

Cover Art: iStock.com/luminouslens

Author Photo: Peggy M. Gordon

Cover Design: Elizabeth Maines McCleavy

Order online: www.finishinglinepress.com
            also available on amazon.com

Author inquiries and mail orders:
Finishing Line Press
P. O. Box 1626
Georgetown, Kentucky 40324
U. S. A.

For my fellow members
of the Working Writers Group,
with deep affection and gratitude

By anarchist spirit I mean that deeply human sentiment, which aims at the good of all, freedom and justice for all, solidarity and love among the people; which is not an exclusive characteristic only of self-declared anarchists, but inspires all people who have a generous heart and an open mind.

—Errico Malatesta, 1922

Anarchism is both a religious faith and a rational philosophy; and many of its anomalies are the product of the clash between the two....

—James Joll, 1964

I

A week after Mother's Day, the gray iron cap of City Hall's tower shimmered in a scorching late-morning sun. At the apex, undaunted by the sky's glare, William Penn—in his 37-foot bronze incarnation—gazed toward the distant northeastern point where he had signed his peace treaty with the Turtle Clan of the Lenape.

Meanwhile, far below his feet, a wide mass of humanity stretched to the west, undulating slowly toward a portable stage. Even if Penn could have turned to view the snaking column, it would have seemed trivial from his lofty perspective, in no way a threat to the peaceable, tolerant, "countrie towne" the founding Quaker had envisioned in 1682.

1

NOT ONE MORE!
—a sign hand-lettered in red, white and blue, lifted high above the marcher's shoulders.

I want to read BOOKS, not EULOGIES
—stark black on white, poked aloft on a wooden cross.

Susie Alioto, a tiny woman packed in by the crowd of marchers on Market Street, strained to see past the welter of signs and banners bouncing around her—what block was this? how much farther to City Hall?—as she proudly hoisted her own handmade contribution, drawn with markers in the anarchist colors of red and black. It aimed straight at the National Rifle Association, which funded the politicians who refused to adopt commonsense gun-control measures. The latest attack in the wave of mass shootings across the country—16 dead, 19 wounded at a high school in the Midwest—had prompted this outpouring into the streets of Philadelphia, semi-coordinated with demonstrations in other cities.

KIDS' BLOOD on YOUR HANDS, NRA!!!!
read Susie's sign, the "blood" red and drippy, the "NRA" a shadowed, ominous black with the outline of a semiautomatic rifle behind it. A longtime teacher as well as activist, Susie knew the value of dramatic presentation.

Through her own local group, TeachPeace, which had helped organize this "Disarm Hate" rally, she'd heard that some Second Amendment supporters—gun rights *nuts*, in her view—planned a countermarch, but so far there was no sign of them, and the only police she'd seen had been calm and cheerful. Though Susie's plans to link up with her friend Margaret had gone awry because of a confusing text message, she didn't mind marching alone. At 66, she was long used to acting on her own when necessary.

As the march progressed, the office buildings grew denser and higher, looming over the wide street, but they failed to block the unseasonably hot sun that bore down on the demonstrators of all ages and colors and ethnicities: two woman in hijabs in front of Susie; a high-stepping, tanned, bearded man in khaki shorts and sandals, carrying his little daughter on his shoulders; an Asian man with a portrait of Gandhi on his T-shirt; a teenage white girl in blue short-shorts and a yellow halter top marching arm in arm with a Black girl in bright orange who would have been Susie's height except for six inches of magnificent Afro. Susie herself wore tan cargo pants and a blue TeachPeace T-shirt.

A chant rippled from the front until everyone joined in, repeating the lines over and over in hypnotic rhythm:

The People, United,
Will Never Be Divided

Dah-DUM-dah, Dah-DUM-dah—the pulse of the crowd lifted Susie, its energy combining with her own outrage at the forces that sacrificed children on the altar of firepower. In the cluster of marchers near her, Susie's was the loudest voice, and she pumped her sign in time with the chant.

Yet the close-packed bodies added to the oppressive heat, and Susie began to feel lightheaded, as if her marching feet down there belonged to someone else. Though she kept her hair in a short, minimum-maintenance cut, clammy gray strands had plastered across her forehead. She'd remembered to wear sunscreen—her olive Italian complexion had paled with the years—but the greasy coating on her cheeks and neck coagulated the sweat. Afraid of stumbling on someone else's feet, she stared at the heels of the bearded man to gauge their distance and simultaneously cussed herself for her weakness.

She'd had a similar sensation, bordering on vertigo, three days ago at her son Eric's college graduation on the Main Line, where the students' relatives had to sit in long rows on an unshaded lawn while the dignitaries enjoyed the shade of the administration building's classical portico. That kind of insensitive elitism had always enraged her, and it was part of what she was protesting here—the stupid arrogance of rich and safe politicians who offered "thoughts and prayers" but no action. So what was wrong with her, wobbling after walking a mere six blocks with a cardboard sign on a lightweight stick?

Susie had more vitality than most people half her age, and a health problem was unusual for her. She took deep, careful breaths, fanned herself with her free hand, brought her sign down to shoulder level to ease her arm. She reminded herself that at the graduation, after that moment of dizziness when she stood up to snap a picture of Eric receiving his diploma, she'd recovered quickly. It was just the heat, for sure.

The marchers slowed, then stopped, except for miscellaneous shuffles and regroupings. The front must have reached City Hall, for between the heads and shoulders Susie glimpsed a makeshift stage, and now a megaphone boomed with another chant:

Hey HEY, ho HO,
The NRA has got to GO

The new thrum of energy gave her a boost, and as she raised her voice she turned to check the signs behind her:

Ban the Piece, Build the Peace
Children or Guns—Why is this even a question?
Even Grandma Is PISSED OFF!!!!

Fuck All Your Guns

The last slogan was lettered over the image of a pistol pointing upward, its barrel morphing into a fat middle finger. Susie appreciated the clever illustration but worried that obscenity played into the hands of the movement's critics.

The crowd jammed the entire pavement between the street-level businesses, mostly law offices, banks, investment houses, accounting firms. To the right, over the sidewalk, she glimpsed the double-interlocking-G logo of GentleGrounds, a small local chain of coffee shops. The logo caught her notice because Eric was starting work for the company on Monday, to earn some cash before he left for grad school on the West Coast. He'd mentioned the shop on Market Street, but she hadn't realized it was in this block, at the base of a fancy office tower. Good for GG, thought Susie—snatching a spot that would normally go to a megacorp like Starbucks.

Then she got caught up in the next echoing chant—

Protect Our Kids

Not Your Guns

—and she thrust her sign high again, bouncing on the balls of her feet while her voice, honed by years in a high school classroom, boomed forth.

As the rhythm died away, the megaphone began to introduce the first speaker, a city councilwoman known for her fiery progressivism. Susie struggled to make out the words through the electronic blur and the commotion of the crowd, which seemed suddenly louder. People around her were jostling, and she pulled her sign down tight against her side as protection against shoulders and elbows. The crowd smelled like what it was, a mass of vibrating, sweaty bodies recently dosed with sunscreen, coffee and scrambled egg.

Then another bullhorn broke in, a more metallic sound, competing with the first voice—

More GUNS

Less CRIME

—and a few people near Susie began to repeat the chant until they realized it was the opposite of what they believed. Shit, that must be the gun rights counterprotesters. Where were they—in front, off to the left? Why weren't the police keeping them away?

The commotion grew as people yelled back in anger. The second amplified voice responded,

An Armed Man Is a Citizen

An Unarmed Man Is a Slave

The first voice uttered instruction: "People, stay calm, they're trying to disrupt us. Officers, officers! We have a permit, they do not! Please control them. Do not let them come up here! Do not let them up here!"

Cheers rang out from the front, and a multitude of shouts—what was happening? Then Susie was knocked in the back. Stumbling, she saw a figure with raised fist fly past her. Clad in tight black pants and T-shirt, with a black hoodie and ski mask, the runner yelled something unintelligible. To Susie's right, another similarly clad person dashed through the crowd, waving a dark object and screaming imprecations against fascists.

These runners looked like Antifa, the Black Bloc, the loosely organized groups famous for direct action in the name of antifascism. Were they heading up front to confront the gun nuts? But that bewildered Susie—why would they show up here? Many of the people she'd met who claimed to be Antifa had no objection to guns per se, feeling they were necessary to fight the evil of white supremacists and other fascists.

Already she was being shoved side to side as ripples spread through the crowd, and she feared worse to come. Using her experience in such situations, she slipped to the right, out of the middle of things. Gaining the sidewalk, she pressed herself against the eight-foot-high window of the GentleGrounds store, where the sun reflected blindingly as she propped her sign in the doorway. This being a Sunday, the store was closed, as were the law firms and bank offices it served.

More shouts up front, angrier, and more amplified blasts, including what seemed to be an official voice, a cop maybe, but there was so much noise it was impossible to know what was happening. The crowd surged forward and back; signs knocked against people's heads; a child fell down and was quickly snatched up by its mother. One of the black-clad sprinters sped back from the front, heading straight at Susie before swerving at the last moment. The slim figure swung something—hammer? tire iron? crowbar?—three, four times at different angles, and the coffee shop's huge window erupted into shards, falling both inward and outward. One splinter clipped Susie's head. A deafening siren rang, and somewhere beneath that clamor a woman's voice wailed.

"Idiot!" Susie tried to holler, but her vocal cords didn't work and the figure was already gone, and when she put her hand to her left ear it came away bloody.

Dizziness hit again as the sun smashed her face. It was time to get out of here. She'd reclaim her sign ... no, too much glass in the way, she'd leave the sign and scoot back along the walls to the first side street ... whoops, she was tilting—needed to stop a minute, how bad was the bleeding? Now she *smelled* it too, the blood.... OW, OW—a knock in the side, crowds are so stupid when they turn into a mob....

4

She was suffocating, she thought, couldn't catch her breath. She tottered, reached for the wall. She fell.

* * *

"Get up, get up!" a voice ordered.

Susie opened her eyes. Had she passed out? For how long? "Lady, hey, hey, come on, the cops are grabbin' people, you don't wanna stay here."

Blocking the sun, a black-hooded head swam over her.

"You're bleeding?!" It was a young woman's voice. "Was it the— Fuck. We've gotta move—they're shutting it down, squads're gonna sweep the street. Lemme see that—over here, turn your head. The fascists try to take over and they'll blame it on us. Just the ear I think but it's bleedin' like fuck. Gimme your arm, can you sit up? That's it, watch your hand, there's glass all over. Wait, I've got something for that."

Slipping off her slim backpack, she pulled out a hunk of gauze and some adhesive tape. "Be prepared, Sean says. Like a joke on the Boy Scout motto?" With quick hands she fashioned a rough bandage for Susie's ear, then yanked the older woman to her feet. "Put your hand here, keep pressure on it, can you do that? … You can walk, can't you?"

Space opened on the street as people hustled back the way the march had come. Miscellaneous voices were yelling. "Disperse quietly," a bullhorn boomed. "People, go home now. There are injuries, we need the street clear for the EMTs."

"Bringing in the paddy wagons, that's what," Susie's companion said, pulling her along. "We saw them lined up on Filbert. They don't give a flying fuck about injuries."

After stumbling at first, Susie was picking up speed, one hand pressed on the bandage, the other arm linked in the young woman's. But her brain floated far above, and it amazed her that her feet and all those other parts down there continued to function when disconnected.

Once they turned a corner, Susie's guide whipped off her black ski mask and hoodie, revealing a white T-shirt and a sheaf of dark hair that fell around her face. She slipped both items of disguise into her backpack. "If anyone asks, you're my mom, we got caught up in the crowd by accident and we're taking you home."

They bore north on 16th Street, and within half a block the congestion dissolved. The noise dwindled behind them. At Race Street the young woman wanted to turn, but Susie shook her arm loose and stopped. This didn't seem right—who was this girl?

"Wait. Where are you pulling me?"

"To my apartment. Few blocks more. Gotta fix that wound. I'm in nursing school, I've got antiseptic and stuff."

Cold sweat chilled Susie's back. Smears of blood stained her T-shirt. "I can get a taxi home," she said uncertainly, "take care of it myself."

"Taxis won't get through right now. For shit sake, let me help. I saw you when that window busted, thought you were okay, then I circled back and you're on the ground."

"Oh." Susie tried to focus. "You broke the window?"

"No! Not me, no…. I saw it, that's all. Some bank windows got hit too."

Steadier now, head reconnecting to her torso, Susie looked up at her rescuer. Tallish, white, with large eyes in a narrow face, a slim athletic body good for pushing through crowds and swinging hammers. About the same age as Susie's son, early twenties.

Though still doubtful, Susie noticed that her ear was throbbing. Antiseptic made sense. Hard to tell how much blood she'd lost; best to have someone look at it.

Her companion was using the pause to check her phone, rapping her fingers on it in impatience. "Where the fuck did he go?" she muttered to herself.

"If I'm your mother," Susie hesitated, "I suppose I should know your name."

"Oh. Yeah, okay. Lauren. That's my real name, actually, not my pseudonym."

"Susie's mine. Also not a pseudonym."

2

By the time they reached the entrance to Lauren's building, Susie's phone was ringing. With effort she dug it out of the thigh pocket on her cargo pants, and when she saw the incoming number through the sweat dripping from her forehead, she answered the call. "Yeah, Eric?"

"Mom! Are you okay! I saw online there's a riot or something!"

"Your social media are being antisocial again, honey. No riot, just the gun nuts acting up and a little breakage by Antifa or somebody. I'm only slightly wounded."

"*Wounded!* Were you attacked? Where are you?"

"I'm with an experienced nurse," Susie lied, "who's going to attend to my superficial cut. I'll be home soon."

"For god sake, Mom, I'll grab a ride share and take you to the hospital! Where are you now—you're still on the street, right? I hear traffic."

"There's no need to come after me, I'm fine. I'll take a bus home. Thank you for your concern, dear, but you don't need to call again. I'll see you soon." After ending the call, she muted her phone.

"Who was that wanting to come get you?" Lauren demanded, frowning. "I was afraid you'd give out the address."

"Why, are you storing explosives here?" Susie raised her eyes to take in the building in front of her.

"*No!* No, it's just—we try to stay anonymous, you know. But we're not Antifa. We support them but we're independent."

It was anonymous enough, this three-story, dirty-brick place on the grungy border of Chinatown. Next to a Thai takeout joint on street level, a stained, four-step stoop led to the apartments above. A double doorbell box, cracked and partially detached, hung by the entrance.

As Lauren mounted the stoop she barked, "Look, there's a cop car down the street, hurry up! Get inside, get *inside*."

She led Susie into a dim, stifling vestibule and clapped the door behind them, panting. "Are you sure that caller's not tracking you?"

"*Tracking* me? Why are you so paranoid?" Susie said.

"I'm not paranoid, just realistic. They'll bust people, interrogate them, beat them, claiming it's for property damage."

"Not likely, if they didn't catch you in the act. The cops in this city have gotten pretty mellow. It's not like the bad old days."

"Mellow?" Lauren puffed, unlocking the inner vestibule door. "They have spy cameras everywhere."

"If you want to know, daughter, that was my son. Calling because he's worried about me. Eric Malatesta Leffler, named after the great Errico, also not a pseudonym."

"The great who? You're babbling now, are you losing more blood? Get upstairs, c'mon, *c'mon.* Third floor—take my arm."

"Let go, I can climb stairs on my own. Why don't you replace that light bulb, it'd be easier to see."

"The landlord won't do fuck."

"It doesn't take a landlord to change a light bulb."

The grimy carpet led them past the second-floor apartment, up another flight to a door set directly atop the staircase, with no landing to stand on. Lauren reached up to unlock a dead bolt, and when the door opened they faced a blank wall. A narrow hallway led left and right. Lauren pointed Susie to the left: "Sit down in the living room, I'll get a washcloth and clean you up."

This top-floor apartment was sweltering, and the window air conditioner Lauren switched on had little immediate effect. Yet the living room felt less dismal than the stairway because it was deep, with windows at front and back, and not overly dirty. Student-type furniture—saggy sofa, cheap IKEA chairs, a chipped white-painted coffee table—surrounded an old TV. Miscellaneous electronics lay scattered about: laptop, tablet, speakers, cords. The worn wooden floor and pale green walls, painted maybe a decade ago, made the place almost quaint. The air smelled faintly, not unpleasantly, like peanut butter.

Susie took a seat on the sofa, and Lauren swooped in with an aluminum bowl of water, washcloth, cotton swabs, a large box of Band-Aids and a tube of antiseptic. "Okay, let's get a close look. I hope you don't need stitches."

"It's throbbing, but I think the bleeding stopped."

The young woman sat beside Susie, her fingers drumming rapidly on her knee. Then she took a deep breath, dipped her head and closed her eyes a few seconds, as if recalibrating.

When she looked up she was less anxious. Her hands moved gently as she removed the temporary bandage on Susie's ear, and Susie thought the claim of nursing school might be true.

"You're right, the flow's almost finished." As Lauren calmed down, her voice dropped to a lower register, with the creaky, crackly tones that Susie heard from many girls in her classroom. Vocal fry, the linguists called it—an affectation in Susie's view, but not the worst possible. "A slice on the lobe, half-inch long, not deep. Whew. It's good you don't wear earrings. When I saw you on the sidewalk, I was like, shit, we didn't want to hurt any little old ladies."

Susie jerked, offended.

"Hold still!"

"I may be short and gray-haired," Susie grumped, "but I'm hardly a 'little old lady.' I do sometimes wear earrings."

"Oh. Didn't mean it that way."

"You're not wearing earrings either."

"No. It's like, the fashion industry, you know, it's part of the whole machinery oppressing women. Who needs it?"

"I agree with that, more or less."

After a soft wash with the cloth, Lauren was dabbing with damp swabs, tossing used ones on the coffee table. Now she switched to antiseptic. "What's that on your T-shirt," she pointed. "TeachPeace."

"Ow, that stings! What do you mean, what's TeachPeace, we helped organize the march! We're teachers, professors, anyone concerned with education for global justice. I was on the board for five years till I rotated off."

"Oh, yeah, right, I saw the list of groups. Bourgeois liberal types."

"That's not fair. And you haven't convinced me it wasn't you that smashed the window."

"It wasn't me, but it's collective action, doesn't matter which individual does the deed."

"It does if the individual is being stupid. I believe in direct action against the state in its material forms, but without a strategic purpose—"

"It's not stupid! We have a purpose! Look, when I finish here, I'll explain our anarchist principles."

"Principles? I've been an anarchist almost five decades, kiddo! Violence at a 'Disarm Hate' rally is not a principle. How much of Malatesta have you read? Voltairine de Cleyre? Rudolf Rocker?"

"Don't know those ..."

"And why do you dress like Antifa if you're not?"

"It's good disguise," Lauren said as she pressed a large Band-Aid into place, and then she turned the tables: "Why do *you* call yourself Susie, a little girl's name?"

"It's always been my name!"

Lauren smirked, her mouth annoyingly close to Susie's face.

"Years ago," Susie went on in self-defense, "some of my friends dropped their nicknames to make the world take them seriously. Like my friend Margie became Margaret. But it's the *world* that ought to change."

"That's for sure."

Lauren sat back, and Susie had a moment to look around the room again. Compared to the anarchist commune where she'd lived as a young woman, this was luxury. The sofa, though well worn, didn't have a single hole in it. Nothing smelled like mildew. The air conditioner was starting to pump out chilled air, cooling the sweat on her forehead.

Before she could ask further questions, steps pounded up the stairs. The door banged open and a man in black burst into the hallway. After slamming to the other side of the apartment, where a thud echoed like something hard tossed onto a closet floor, he stormed into the living room.

"For fuck sake, where did you go?" Lauren blurted.

He was tall, slender—a long face with a sharp nose, long arms, wide thin lips and a pale complexion. About Lauren's age. Before paying any attention to her, he ripped off his black hoodie to reveal a hairy chest and flat stomach, then peeled off his latex gloves. He was drenched from his matted straight brown hair to his cropped mustache to his pallid torso. He threw the excess clothing on the floor. "Fucking cops," he griped, "grabbing anyone in black, me and Maxie went way around to lose them."

"Congratulations on your escape," Susie said. "Except that by running to your own door with your disguise on, you let everyone on the street know a radical lives here. And the way you crashed in, you made sure everyone noticed."

"Who the fuck," he glared at Susie and Lauren, "is *this*?"

"She got cut when you—you know, when that big store window got broken?"

"She *what*? Nobody got cut—"

"Yeah, she did. I cleaned her up."

"Fucking shit, she could be a spy!"

"No! Don't go fucking off your head on this. She's just a little old lady that was on the march, that's all."

"I am *not*," Susie insisted, "just a little old lady *or* a spy, and since you can't say three words without cursing, I won't burden you any longer with my presence. Thank you, Lauren, for your assistance."

When Susie stood up from the sofa, the man clapped his hands on her shoulders and shoved her down again.

"You *stay* there till we find out who you are!"

Susie scowled angrily. Since he reminded her of a certain type of student she'd had in her classes, skinny boys who verged on the ridiculous when they tried to assert masculine control, she had little fear of him. "My name is Susie Alioto," she snapped. "I'm a teacher and a member of TeachPeace"—she pointed to the logo on her shirt—"which helped organize the march you so royally screwed up."

"Huh," he laughed sarcastically. "Collaborationists. Getting permits from the city and all that legal shit."

"There's nothing wrong with having city approval for a march, it keeps the cops out of your face unless you get violent. Smashing windows is a dumb tactic—especially a local coffee shop that wasn't harming anyone—but I'm not on the side of the fascists or the police. So you can stop behaving like a world-class asshole."

His eyes wavered; he took an uncertain step toward Susie and then moved quickly to the front windows to pull down the blinds.

"And you don't have to be paranoid," Susie added. "Nobody can see in on such a bright day."

"Sean, she's right, relax."

"Coffee shops," he sneered. "Hangouts for latte liberals, we don't need 'em."

"Before you ran away, did you see how many people got hurt?" Susie quizzed him. "Did the gun nuts start fights?"

"How should I know?"

"All right then, I'm leaving now," Susie declared, standing up again. "I won't report you or reveal your address. I'd say it was nice to meet you, Sean, but it wasn't."

He slid over to block her exit, his eyes contracting. "How the fuck do you know my name?" he challenged.

"Because Lauren just said it!"

"Yeah, I did, Sean, actually."

After a deep breath, he relented, almost deflated. "All right," he mumbled. "Look, we have to be careful. I don't mean to be rude."

"No, you *do* mean it, but I understand the situation. Your tactics may be foolish, but as I told Lauren, I've been part of the movement since before you were born. I won't give you away."

"Are you okay to get home?" Lauren sounded genuinely concerned. She'd risen and moved to Susie's side.

"I can get a bus. I'm just up in Fairmount."

"That's some bougie-ass neighborhood for someone in the *movement*," Sean pointed out.

"You seem to have a lot of prejudices," Susie countered. "Years ago, when I moved in, it was mostly working class. Now, I admit, we have a couple of *coffee shops*."

"Give me your phone number. I want to check on you," said Lauren.

"Why?" Sean frowned.

"That's nice of you, dear, but I'm sure I'll be fine. If there's any infection I'll see a doctor."

Undeterred, Lauren whipped out her phone, and Susie recited her number, not sure this was a good idea. Sean stood to the side, angled away from the women.

Though Susie ought to try to educate these people, she didn't look forward to further contact.

3

When he heard his mother crunch open the front door, which stuck in humid weather, Eric stomped downstairs, furious.

"Mom, why did you hang up on me? And when I called back you didn't answer! What happened? How bad are you hurt?"

A gangly 22-year-old, well over six feet and scarcely 150 pounds, with longish, untamed brown curls, Eric looked the part of a new college graduate: torn jeans, dirty T-shirt, perpetual slouch. However, as the winner of his college's math award and a full fellowship to the Ph.D. program at the University of Washington, he felt he carried a certain authority, which his mother had not yet acknowledged.

She ignored his questions and proceeded through the living room into the kitchen, where she sat by the air conditioner and fanned her face.

"Is that a bandage on your ear?" he persisted, following her. "There's blood all over your shirt!"

"Yes, Eric, it's just a scratch. I bled a bit, that's all. There was some scuffling up front, I was nowhere near it." She sighed. "What's the latest report from your antisocial media?"

"You mean about the march? Fights between rival groups, police breaking it up, arrests."

"It was the gun nuts lying in wait for us."

"Yeah, right, your people are never to blame, are they?"

"Not when we plan a peaceful, legal march, no."

"How did you get blood all over if it was so peaceful?"

"A few militants moved in, started busting things. I'm afraid they broke the glass at your new job."

"Huh?"

"The GentleGrounds store on Market. You should call tomorrow before you go in, find out if they're going to open. It's a big front window they'll have to replace."

"Jesus, Mom!"

"Jesus wasn't there. He'd probably duck responsibility anyway."

Typical of his mother—this refusal to take his objections seriously. What Eric saw, in the tile-floored kitchen of their small two-story row house, was a woman who'd seemed to age rapidly during his four years of college. Maybe it was just being away for most of the school year, visiting home only once a month or so, that let him notice the changes. Her wavy hair had grayed, and of course she was too "authentic" to dye it or to wear makeup. Her shoulders had begun to curve slightly into a stoop. Though she claimed to have no medical conditions except for slightly high blood pressure, for which she'd taken pills for years, he worried about her.

At 66, she was exactly three times his age. Their ages and the gap between made an interesting mathematical progression: 22, 44, 66, all double numerals, evenly spaced, and all three being Størmer numbers. 44 was also a tribonacci number, and 22 and 66 were both Erdős–Woods numbers. Many other fascinating characteristics occurred to him, drawing his mind into spirals of speculation.... But the point was: his mother was growing old.

Right now, she looked spent from the march, the injury, the heat, as she leaned toward the air vent, her face damp and saggy. The blood on her T-shirt upset him, and he wondered if he should have accompanied her to the rally. She'd invited him—"You've got nothing else to do on Sunday, Mr. Honors Graduate, you should come out of gratitude that your own campus hasn't been shot up"—but he wasn't an activist, and once he'd passed the age when she could drag him along, he'd refused to pretend an interest. Nobody favored students' getting murdered, but what good did marches do? Also, since the unforgettable antiwar rally when he was eight years old, when she'd taken the megaphone to introduce him as her son named after a famous anarchist, he'd developed a deep aversion to the type of idealists who'd applaud such nonsense.

He himself hated his middle name, Malatesta. At age 13 one of his friends teased him that it meant "diseased testicle," which upset him until he went online to check. Actually, it meant "bad head," Italian slang for a treacherous person—hardly better. The fact that a family named Malatesta had ruled Rimini for two centuries didn't appease him. Nor did he like being linked to an ideology he didn't share. Yes, he was kind of left-wing like his friends, but anarchist?—no way. He'd never understood how the "voluntary" and "cooperative" social order that anarchists favored wouldn't soon come to resemble the "state" they wanted to dismantle.

As for the Errico Malatesta poster over there on the side of the refrigerator—on which the scruffy-bearded, wild-haired hero looked more than half crazed—Eric had learned not to see it.

Maybe, though, he should have gone on the march today just to watch over Susie. Slumped in her chair to catch the cool air, she looked fragile, delicate—and these were words that, a few years ago, he couldn't have conceived applying to his fierce little mother.

"One good thing," he said. "You didn't get tear-gassed this time."

"No, the police were well-behaved. At least until fighting broke out—I couldn't see what they did then. Maybe some are on our side on this issue; they don't like ordinary citizens walking around with assault weapons and armor-piercing bullets."

"There's some video online, looks like a mad scramble. You'll see it on your TV news tonight."

"If the news can be trusted. Usually not."

He noted her "maybe" and "usually," and these words signaled one of his other objections to Susie's politics—that she wasn't half as radical as she pretended. Though she worshiped historical rebels who'd committed, or at least condoned, political assassinations, her own protests were entirely peaceful. Though she claimed the government was inherently oppressive, she voted in every election, reliably Democratic, never deviating to the Green Party or the Socialists who weren't going to win anyway. She hung out with organizations like TeachPeace, full of middle-class white professionals. Worse, she'd taught for decades at Hubble Day School, a prestigious private institution populated by the economic elite, and with her big faculty discount she'd enrolled Eric there from kindergarten through high school, giving him the excellent education that led to his scholarship at a private college and now his high-powered grant for grad school. This outcome was fine with him, naturally, but in his view she was hypocritical, or to put it more nicely, her bite didn't match her bark. The "bourgeois anarchist," he called her—privately, except for one time he'd said it to her face as a joke, which she didn't take kindly. She was so serious about her "principles," but in the last election—when he had forced himself to vote for the first time, mainly because she wouldn't let him forget—her ballot had matched his exactly.

It sucked, having to deal with her contradictions, and they'd have to share the house all summer till he left for Washington. He ground his teeth at the thought. And yet, a minute later, he was startled to see her fumble.

Getting up to fetch herself some water, she'd bobbled the glass at the sink, and then banged her knee in recovering it. Would she be okay alone when he left?

"Mom, sit, let me get that! You're exhausted. Why don't you go upstairs and lie down awhile?"

"Thank you, dear, but the American people have been lying down too long. Two cubes of ice, if you don't mind. That's a big help."

4

The early-evening TV news coverage was fairer than Susie expected, describing the march as peaceful until "fistfights" erupted with the counter-protesters and "a squad of black-suited radicals" attacked store windows and parked cars. A few people had been taken to hospital, though no major injuries were reported. Four arrests had been made, it wasn't clear who. Martha Gupta, a leader of Children First! and spokesperson for the marchers, decried the gun nuts as "right-wing hatemongers," and a police captain blamed "outside agitators and hoodlums that sow chaos." Phoning Margaret Pasicznyk, the friend she'd failed to connect with at the march because of confusing text messages, Susie learned that none of her own group had been detained or hurt except for Susie's minor wound, which Margaret was surprised to hear about. Overall, not as bad as it could have been, and it seemed the message of the rally wasn't being overwhelmed by the media sensationalism.

After she and Eric shared a pizza for dinner, he holed up in his room, probably absorbed in video games or role-playing sites, with his favorite brand of noise music (which he said was called "mathcore"—was he putting her on?) blasting in his earbuds. To her, the video games were just explicit cartoon violence, and the music sounded like hamsters being crucified.

Susie headed to bed early, missing the late news, so the next morning when she fetched her paper from the stoop—she still subscribed to the dwindling print edition—she was startled by a front-page story about a child hurt in the "riot." Scuffing to the kitchen in her bathrobe and slippers, she located her reading glasses and scanned the story and photo captions while, with her free hand, she started to measure coffee into the grinder. In warm weather she brewed plenty so she could have it iced later in the day.

Wait a minute—that picture?! It was the splintered front window of GentleGrounds! She could see the logo above the broken glass.

Abandoning the coffee, she flumped down heavily at the table.

Boy, 4, Sustains Serious Injury in Riot

Six weeks ago, a proud Rita Gutierrez cut the ribbon on the third in her small chain of GentleGrounds coffee shops. The new store a block from Dilworth Park in the shadow of City Hall, aimed to serve the bustling Center City crowds of businesspeople, officeworkers, commuters, and shoppers. It was Gutierrez's initial venture into a major commercial corridor, and the first weeks of operation proved every bit as successful as she hoped.

Now, after the rampage that erupted Sunday during the Disarm Hate march, she sits by the hospital bed of her heavily bandaged four-year-old son, Mateo.

The store's large front window, shattered during the riot, sent shards of glass flying into the little boy's face. In addition to deep cuts on his cheeks and forehead, his right eye was damaged. After emergency surgery, with further procedures to come, doctors at Children's Hospital remain uncertain whether the sight in the eye can be saved.

"Those people, they went wild," said Gutierrez, shaking her head angrily. "Our store was closed, like always on Sunday, it's a business district, you know? But they said the street'll be full with protesters, so I went in to see it's locked up tight because I was in a rush when I left Saturday."

She took her little boy, she explained, because he has no preschool or babysitter on Sundays. "We were going to leave right away, but by then there's so many outside, we waited, we saw all these people waving signs. And then it's like, the glass just explodes in our face."

Gutierrez called 911 but response was slow. "I ran blocks and blocks carrying him and finally we got a cab, he took us to the hospital."

As a mother Gutierrez cannot fathom violence toward children. Nor, as the owner of a small business, can she understand why her store was targeted.

"Our schools have to be safe. People want to march for it, that's good. But why destroy? 'Disarm Hate,' they say. Is it a joke or what? Why attack us? My baby, he's scarred for life, and maybe he'll never see right."

In one of the color photos, white bandages hid most of the bedridden child's face. The mother, a slim, dark-haired woman, looked no older than Eric. On the newsprint the walls of the hospital room appeared a ghastly greenish tan, punctuated by the harsh metal sheen of the overbed table.

Susie tasted nausea in her throat.

First she reacted to the personal aspects of the story, the innocent child traumatized, his life maybe ruined. Then the social: a young Latina woman (a single mother like Susie herself?) trying to build a respectable business but whacked by savagery. Then the political: a stain on the entire movement for peace, human rights, tolerance, safety … a child mutilated on the very day they were protesting children being shot!

And behind all this, the similarity to another injury from long ago, one she never wanted to think about, one that made a cramp around her heart.

Spinning away from that memory, she flushed with rage at the idiocy of those black-suited pretend-anarchist jackasses. As both a practitioner and a teacher—in her commune days, she'd taught anarchist theory and history—she couldn't abide such behavior.

She glanced at the poster on the side of her refrigerator, positioned so she could see it from where she always sat. Curling at the edges, stained with specks of tomato sauce, it never ceased to comfort her: a portrait of Malatesta in his later years against a dramatic field of red and black, combined with a quote of his she especially liked, "Impossibility never prevented anything from happening"—inspirational at the darkest times. A subtle thinker about combining the necessity of revolution with respect for human life, he'd agree with her on the brainlessness of these young window-breakers. She'd often discussed such matters with him over the decades, but right now she was too upset for chat.

Susie forgot her coffee, forgot breakfast—though she always lectured Eric about its importance—and brooded. Her wounded ear throbbed. After half an hour she called her school to say she'd be taking a sick day, which she hated doing. Then, mechanically, she tromped back upstairs, showered and dressed, changed her Band-Aid. She lay down, still angry and depressed, and sank into a sticky, troubled doze. It was almost 9 o'clock when she woke, recalling that Eric was supposed to start work today.

At his bedroom door, she rapped her fist beside the sign he'd designed and printed for himself: "Do Not Disturb" in huge letters atop a futuristic battle scene featuring robots and scantily clad nymphs. The predominant colors, red and black, struck her as a parody of the anarchist flag.

"Eric," she yelled. "When are you supposed to be at the coffee shop? Did you call to see if they're open today? The owner's little boy got hurt! Eric, are you awake? I'm coming in."

As she reached for the handle the door wrenched inward. "Mom!" he yelped. "What *is* it?" He was dressed in a ragged T-shirt, boxer shorts and a five-inch yawn. His curly hair wandered as spectacularly as ever, and his pale complexion had darkened under the cheekbones.

"You look hung over, how late were you playing online?… Never mind, aren't you going to work today? What time were you supposed to start?"

"I don't know, 10 o'clock? What time is it now?"

"Late, you need to get a move on. Unless they're staying closed, I don't know."

"Okay, uh...." He yawned again. "So, um, you want me to conform to the work schedules of the capitalist hierarchy." He offered a lazily sarcastic grin.

"No, Eric, it's a little coffee shop, not a hierarchy. I want you to conform to your promises and responsibilities. But Mateo Gutierrez was seriously hurt yesterday by the glass."

"Who's Mateo Gutierrez? What glass?"

"The little son of your new boss! When the store window broke, I told you!"

"Oh?" He tilted his head to the left. "How do you know this?"

Explanations followed, and Eric eventually agreed to locate the number he'd been given for his new employer and find out whether he should report for work. Scratching his butt, he closed his bedroom door. Susie wandered downstairs and stared once more at the newspaper.

On impulse, she located her phone, an old, small, bright-red device, and dialed Miriam Schneiderman, a retired principal and current director of TeachPeace.

"Miriam, it's Susie. Sorry to bother you. You saw the newspaper? The front page?"

"Oh. Yeah. My husband showed me online. The story's been picked up nationally, I'm afraid. Anti-gun rally gone bad, that kind of overblown rhetoric. We're putting out a statement disavowing the violence, Naomi's drafting it. The way those gun fanatics attacked us, it was criminal. The other participating groups are issuing press releases too, and Martha spoke to the media yesterday."

"Yeah, I heard Martha on TV. Shouldn't we say something specific about little Mateo?"

"Who?"

"The four-year-old that nearly lost his eye. Or maybe did lose his sight. The same window that slashed my ear, but I didn't see them."

"Wait ... your ear?"

"Didn't you hear? I got cut when they smashed the window at Gentle-Grounds—a minor thing, didn't need a doctor. But she was—this little boy, he and his mother must've been right inside when the glass shattered."

"It sounds terrible. I'm so sorry you were hurt, Susie. Are you okay now?"

"I'm fine. But what about the boy? I feel like we should address that directly, maybe speak to the mother. Because in the news article she was blaming the movement."

"We're making clear," Miriam said firmly, "that none of the violence was our doing. It wasn't TeachPeace, it wasn't Children First!—none of the organizing groups. We're committed to nonviolent protest. It was the gun rights hooligans that started fights."

"Actually it was some people dressed like Antifa that broke windows. Of course it wasn't our members, but it hurts, I mean it feels so wrong when this young Latina mother thinks we're responsible for a, a tragedy that ..."

"We're making clear," Miriam emphasized again, "that we don't condone any form of violence. Peace is in our *name*, for god sake. But to isolate any one individual that was hurt, that would only give the distorted stories more play in the media. That little boy, he was apparently the only *serious* injury, and our enemies would love to exaggerate what happened and pretend it was our fault, that protest leads to lawlessness."

"Right," said Susie. "Still ..."

Though the conversation continued for a couple of minutes, Susie wasn't sure what she wanted to express, and she grew increasingly frustrated. After hanging up, she continued to brood while she finished grinding coffee and setting up the pot.

An assault maiming a little boy—such a random horror! An awful byproduct of twisted principles! In the context of the anti-violence rally, a savage irony!

Worse, in some ways this seemed a universal evil thumbing its nose at the marchers' good intentions—because Susie, despite her atheism and her long dedication to political hope, sometimes feared, like the early French anarchist Proudhon, that Original Sin might actually exist, at least as part of the human mind.

Then she had to pee, so she ducked into the powder room off the kitchen. She could hear the shower running upstairs, a probable sign that Eric intended to go somewhere rather than play video games or read sci-fi/fantasy trash all day. In the little mirror over the sink, she noticed the silly appearance of the Band-Aid wrapping her left ear lobe.

After the failure of yesterday's protest—for "failure" now seemed a correct label—the image in the mirror upset her. It wasn't just the Band-Aid: with Susie's gray hair and yellowish teeth, plus her slightly olive complexion that turned sallow in the fluorescent bathroom light, she resembled a bag lady lurking in a downtown alley.

She thought of that girl's remark about the "little old lady" and also of the fact that her baby boy was now a college graduate. She remembered Eric's odd rant three months ago on his birthday, something about their ages being double digits separated by another double digit, a bit of mathematical trivia evidently meant to stress how ancient she was. Having given birth at age 44, she'd always been sensitive about being older than the other parents in his nursery school, his kindergarten—all the way up through high school. She'd taken care to do for him everything that other mothers did for their kids, and more: music lessons (he played an enthusiastic, tuneless trumpet), Little League (he struck out far too often), museum visits (where his boredom made him cranky), summer camp (a financial strain but she managed).

But—no use pretending now, she was old. Glaring at the countenance in the mirror, she also pondered her dizzy weakness in the heat the past few days. At Eric's graduation she'd flopped down in her chair when the wooziness came over her, and in that moment, under the broiling sun among a horde of happy people she didn't know, she'd felt empty, washed out. Her friend Margaret, who'd known Eric since infancy, had hoped to come to the ceremony but had opted instead for a grandson's sixth birthday in Baltimore, so Susie sat alone with her thoughts. Eric was heading thousands of miles away to grad school. Susie's other family responsibility, her parents, had both died more than five years ago in a suburban nursing home. Of her three siblings, all older than she, two had died of heart disease in their early sixties, and the other had crossed to the dark side, becoming a hedge fund manager in San Francisco. So now, with the whole family departed in one way or another, what would be left for Susie?

This sad meditation had persisted when she took Eric out for a graduation dinner, during which he gobbled approximately ten pounds of barbecued ribs and recited, in excruciating detail, the plot of the latest fantasy novel he'd read, oblivious to her depression.

Of course she knew she still had plenty to do in life—her students, her friends, her activism—yet as she scowled at the mirror, her pulsing ear and slack cheeks mocked such evasions. She also knew, through her social conscience, that moping about one's irrelevance was mostly a First World luxury, but somehow this realization didn't cheer her up. With its deep lines and pouches, the face staring back at her looked as played-out as peace marches in a society that adored violence.

After all, she'd passed what the government called retirement age, so maybe she should just retire, from everything. Who would care, or even notice? This was such a self-destructive notion that it felt good, like biting down on a sore tooth.

Shutting the light on the ugly face in the glass, she went to pour herself a cup of coffee, her first sustenance of the day. It tasted bitter, suiting her mood, but her introspection was broken by Eric's crashing down the stairs (he seldom *walked* down stairs). Mug in hand, she intercepted him at the front door.

"Where are you off to in such a rush?"

"My job. Remember?" His hair, wet and matted from a shampoo, looked neater and straighter than usual.

"The store's open today?"

"Yeah yeah, I talked to some guy, he said they boarded up the big window and it looks awful but they're open for business."

"That's good. Do you want, at least, a cup of coffee before you run?"

"I'm going to a *coffee* shop, Mom. And my shift starts in 32 minutes!"

"Okay.... Wait! Wait a sec." She set her cup on the radiator cover and bit her lip, thinking hard.

"What now? ... Mother, I'm going to be la-ate!" he sing-songed, spreading his long arms like a condor trying to take off.

Her depression did three acrobatic flips and wrenched itself inside out. "I'm coming with you," she decided.

"No you're not! My first day, I'm not walking in with my *mother*!"

"I have to talk to them, that's all. Nobody will know I'm with you. When's the next bus?"

5

It was indeed ugly, Susie thought, the sheets of plywood nailed over the gaping hole where the store's front window had been. Otherwise, Market Street appeared unaffected by yesterday's so-called riot. The gates of delivery trucks clanged; pedestrians scurried this way and that; a garage entrance beeped as a car emerged; brakes squeaked or squealed; smokers congregated near office tower entrances; the smells of tobacco, exhaust, dust, cologne and breakfast sandwiches mingled. If not for the plywood evidence, the political ruckus might have been a dream.

Inside, with the window blocked and overhead lights on, the morning felt oddly like nighttime. The place had a sleekly modern decor: two dozen glass-topped tables with slender black fiberglass bases, metal-frame chairs with black vinyl seats and backs. Yet the seating was arranged in what seemed like informal clumps, perhaps intended to promote conversation rather than isolated laptop use. Susie doubted, though, that customers in a commercial district would pay much attention to one another, and at this hour the modest number of customers had scattered as widely as possible.

Two baristas, a young man and woman in black GentleGrounds T-shirts, worked behind the counter and display cases. The air conditioning, already running strong, hit Susie with a refreshing blast after the humid bus ride. Odors of roasted coffee and nutmeg wafted.

Susie hung back while Eric approached the counter and was referred to a man who appeared to be the manager. After a few minutes, when Eric disappeared into the rear, she approached the man. He was of medium height, broad, with a wide flat nose, gray hair around a large bald spot, spreading jowls and a dark-cream complexion. "Hello," she said. "Do you have a minute? I'm Susie Alioto. Eric's mother actually, but I came in for a chance to speak with the manager. How are you?" She held out a hand, which the man hesitated before shaking briefly.

"Joe Sambucco. Is there a problem with your son? He need special treatment or something? I didn't know a new guy was starting, we're kinda messed up on account of the vandals."

"No, no, it's not about Eric. I wanted to say ... ," and she paused because she was still working it out, "I was here yesterday, in the march, and I"—she thought to point at her bandage—"I was hurt, too, when the window broke."

"Lady, it wasn't our fault!" he expostulated, crossing his arms. "It was hoodlums! The store was closed!"

He was dressed in suit pants and an open-collared white shirt with sleeves rolled up, exposing forearms almost comically furry.

"Oh no," said Susie, "I didn't mean— I just wanted, I saw the story about the owner's little boy, his eye, and I wanted to express our sympathy. I'm a member of TeachPeace, one of the organizations behind the march—not on the board anymore, not officially speaking for them—but at least to say, um, I personally am so, so *sorry*, as a mother first of all, that violent people took advantage of the situation ..."

"Your ear cut bad?" Joe Sambucco asked, unfolding the hairy arms.

"No, I'm fine, just a nick, but little Mateo, I read ..."

"Matty's whole face got sliced up. His eye was practically out of his head."

"Ooh," she grimaced.

"But he's at Children's, the best eye doctors.... Look, I got nothing against your demonstration thing yesterday, only the asses that busted stuff."

"Good, I'm glad you see the difference between peaceful protest and—"

"Don't know how it's gonna help, cutting down gun sales when you got so many criminals packing already."

"It's a complicated issue. Anyway, if you ... next time you communicate with the owner, Ms. Gutierrez, could you let her know that someone stopped in to—to express support and, uh, sympathy?"

"She's getting all kinds of support. From our family."

"Your family?"

"She's my niece."

"Oh." This puzzled Susie, who hadn't considered that a Latina woman might have an uncle with an Italian name. At once she was embarrassed, afraid she'd betrayed some kind of ethnic stereotyping. "Oh," she stumbled, "so you're here ... helping out with ..."

"I'm like her silent partner, financial guy, handle the books. I told Rita, you stay with Matty in the hospital, I'll watch the stores. So I got a couple buddies, we came over yesterday, swept the glass, nailed up those boards—which oughta be the building super's job but I wasn't gonna wait on him. Then I came in today too because there's no morning manager yet, Rita's been here everyday herself. I can tell you one thing: No goons are gonna shut her down, I won't stand for it. She's worked too hard for this."

"That's very good of you."

He shrugged. "It's my business too. This new store's going so good, I don't wanta miss a week. Besides, the rent here's humongous, you can't take days off."

"I guess not. Well, thank you, Mr. Sambu—"

"Joe. Call me Joe. You're Susie, you said?"

"Yes. And if you think of it, when there's a progress report for Matty, you could mention it to Eric and he'll pass it on to—"

"I'm calling Rita this afternoon, I'll let you know. Just gimme your number. You didn't need to come in here today, I appreciate it. I believe you're a lady that cares about doing the right thing."

"I do care, yes. Which sometimes gets me in trouble."

He pulled out his phone and punched in her information. "Alioto? Good name," he smiled. Then he shook her hand again, more personally this time. His mitt was large and damp.

As she was turning away, Eric sloped out of the back room in an untucked GentleGrounds T-shirt that billowed around his skinny frame.

"One other thing, Susie," Joe muttered.

"Yes?"

"This son of yours. Does he ever comb his hair?"

Now dry, Eric's curls had sproinged up again in random directions.

"That *is* combed, I'm afraid," said Susie.

6

On the bus home from the coffee shop, Susie's spirits improved. If the "best eye doctors" at Children's were taking care of Matty, maybe his sight would be saved. And since his uncle, who had a huge reason to be angry, understood that the gun-control movement wasn't to blame, perhaps the inflated media coverage wouldn't damage the cause.

Personally, though, Susie remained uneasy, in part because she'd marched into that shop without taking care to present herself right. Remembering the old lady in the mirror, she critiqued her green blouse and saggy jeans. She hadn't washed her hair—was it any neater than Eric's? What had that Joe Sambucco seen, the same kind of gray mouse that Lauren scoffed at? With a dumb bandage on her ear?

As she watched the overweight woman across the bus aisle fish a candy bar from a giant purse, another worry popped up: Had she embarrassed Eric by arriving with him at a new job? She hadn't identified herself to anyone but Joe, who understood her purpose. Still, Eric might have felt— Oh hell, he was immune to most forms of social embarrassment, Susie was convinced, because he paid so little attention.... No, if she'd shamed anyone it was herself, with her baggy old jeans and clumsy explanations.

These personal mortifications meant so little in the big picture, she shouldn't get distracted....

Yet as she stepped off the bus onto a glaring street corner, the personal swelled up and smacked her: five long seconds of lightheadedness and blurred vision before she found the curb. Arms thrown out for balance, eyes averted from the shimmering hot sky—just a block and a half to her own stoop, but sweat slimed her face by the time she wobbled on the steps and bumbled with her key.

Inside, she drank a tall glass of iced coffee and rested in a kitchen chair before deciding she might nap before lunch. It was good she'd called in sick today because she might actually *be* sick. An early summer flu?

She woke in her bed at 2:17, fully dressed and sticky in the creases, groggy and drained. She dragged herself downstairs and forced herself to eat a tomato and lettuce sandwich for lunch, which she realized was also her breakfast. Two more glasses of iced coffee helped perk her up.

Afterward, she fetched her laptop to look up GentleGrounds. Across her screen splashed bright images of yummy snacks (were those cream-filled brownie cookies!?), stylish store interiors, glistening coffee machines. A full section described the philosophy and techniques of coffee roasting, which to

Susie meant little, but she appreciated the commitment to "ethical trade" in purchase of beans. Then she located the "Our Staff" page, which featured head shots of employees at all three locations—a nice touch. She followed the link to a page on "Our Founder," which included a photo of Rita Gutierrez smiling prettily in an apron with the GG logo. The short bio. described her as a graduate of a high-rated culinary college in Delaware, "passionate" about "wholesome artisanal" foods as well as "ecologically and socially responsible" sourcing. No spouse was mentioned, nor was Uncle Joe.

At this point Susie sat back on the sofa, closed the laptop and faced—with great reluctance—the ethical question that had festered in the back of her mind since she saw the morning newspaper.

The strike on the store window was no longer a mere attack on capitalist property. It had caused grave injury to an innocent boy and his family. Susie's gut called it a crime. And Susie knew the probable perpetrator—that insolent kid Sean, or one of his small cell of pseudo-anarchists. (Since Lauren had never heard of Malatesta, Susie refused to consider them real anarchists.)

So: should she contact the police?

For Susie this was a loaded question—more loaded than an assault weapon with a high-capacity magazine.

For more than a century anarchists had debated the role of violence in the fight against the overbearing state. Since the state itself was violent by nature—suppressing freedom and oppressing the people in order to perpetuate control by the ruling classes—armed revolution was almost certainly inevitable. In the meantime, attacks on particularly heinous oppressors could be justified, according to many theorists. Yet indiscriminate savagery was not.

Take the great American anarchist Voltairine de Cleyre. When she heard about the assassination of a Spanish prime minister, a malefactor who'd ordered the torture of innocent socialists and unionists, she leapt to the assassin's defense. Yet the same de Cleyre argued again and again for peace. "Every act of violence finds its echo in another act of violence," she wrote.

Malatesta himself often weighed in on the subject, distinguishing between "the intelligent act of a man who, before acting, weighs the probable good or evil that may result for his cause, and the thoughtless act of the man who strikes at random."

So: wasn't it "random" to bust a coffee shop window into a child's face?

On the other hand, collaborating with cops was anathema. As the watchdogs of wealth (de Cleyre's phrase), the police routinely protected the rich by beating down on poor people, Blacks, gays, radicals. Understanding this, a true anarchist like Emma Goldman refused "to invoke the law against anybody, no matter how great his villainy." Today, even mild liberals knew that if you saw an African American shoplifting, you shouldn't summon law enforcement unless you wanted the person shot. Many cops needed even less excuse: driving while Black; assisting another motorist while Black; walking after dark while Black—anything could get you executed on site. Malatesta wrote at one point, "To me a policeman is worse than a criminal."

Though Susie had no personal rancor against cops, she'd long held to this philosophy. Soon after she bought her house, for instance, she'd been mugged on the sidewalk, her purse snatched. Not for a moment—well, maybe a few minutes—did she consider reporting the incident. The perpetrator was a Black teen who probably needed the money more than she did. Though for days she walked around bruised and furious, she wouldn't give the cops another excuse to harass young people of color.

All this formed the background of Susie's mental debate, to which she added, in a somewhat incoherent jumble, these further thoughts: (a) Though Lauren and Sean might be misguided, they hadn't intended to hurt the little boy. (b) On principle, a revolutionary should never be a snitch. (c) And yet, so-called anarchists stupid enough to attack a harmless coffee shop—a local one, not a national chain—might *deserve* to get busted, to teach them a lesson! Especially since the child's injury was all too reminiscent of the one she didn't want to reminisce about....

It was enough to cause a headache, and Susie felt one coming on. She closed her eyes, leaned back, tried to relax, but the soft burr of air conditioning gave way to booming thumps. She jerked to attention. Was someone jackhammering the sidewalk? Or a car backfiring?

After a pause the thumps came again, and now she identified the source: her front door. She lurched to her feet and stumbled around the coffee table.

When she spotted the problem through the glass of the door's upper panels, she trembled. This was scary—way too much of a coincidence.

But she put on a defiant face and yanked the door open. "The bell works," she pointed. "You don't have to rattle the whole neighborhood."

The two people in short-sleeved, collared shirts and newish slacks squinted up from the sidewalk as if they had nothing to do with the commotion, but it was clear what they were, even before they flashed badges.

"So, can I help you?" Susie made herself go on, while her stomach churned and her eyes contracted against the sunlight.

"Susan Alioto?"

"Wait," Susie hesitated. "Don't I know you? Aren't you ... Officer Tate?"

"Detective Tate now," the policewoman said.

31

7

Five years before, a Black Lives Matter march had streamed up Broad Street to protest police killings of unarmed Black men. In the midst of the column, Susie led a cohort of a dozen people recruited from her friends and TeachPeace colleagues, a group that stood out because they were mostly light-skinned and female. A few police were present to keep the marchers on the sidewalks, and everything went smoothly, except at one major intersection where the long line of activists held up traffic. Drivers honked and swerved; some yelled out their windows, either in support or frustration; the one young cop in the intersection made things worse by giving hand signals that contradicted the stoplights.

When Susie's group reached the crossing, she felt a hand clamp her arm. "Hold up, ma'am," a voice said, and as Susie turned to see who had stopped her, the placard in her right hand—

WHITE SILENCE IS VIOLENCE

—swung left and lightly nicked the top of the person's head.

"Ow!" said the policewoman. "Watch that thing!" Short-haired, late-thirtyish, African American, a couple of inches taller than Susie, she packed her uniform solid.

"Sorry. What's—why did you grab me?"

"Tryin' to keep you safe! Somebody almost got hit a minute ago. Let the street clear. They put a guy out there—a good officer but he's got no clue about traffic."

"My group needs to keep up with the rest," Susie insisted.

"You'll catch up.... Are these your people?" The officer scanned the clump of marchers jammed at the edge of the sidewalk.

Susie nodded and pointed to her shirt.

"TeachPeace?" asked the officer. "What's that?"

"People who believe in education for global justice."

"Big subject, sister. Good luck with *that*."

The wry face made Susie chuckle. "Progress may be slow," she answered, "but we've got to keep fighting."

"I hear you," said the officer. "And your sign is true. Just be careful with it, would you? Don't bash us innocent bystanders."

Whether this was a joke or not—the police as innocent bystanders in a march against police brutality—Susie didn't know. But reading the nameplate on the blue shirt, she smiled and said, "Thanks for your help, Officer Tate."

* * *

Now, half a decade later, Susie didn't know whether Tate would re-member their earlier encounter, but it might help to remind her. "We've met before. About five years ago, at a Black Lives Matter march."

Tate offered a noncommittal but not-totally-unfriendly nod.

Her companion, a crew-cut young blond guy whose shirt strained over a muscular chest, snorted at the mention of Black Lives Matter. Removing his baseball cap to mop his brow with a forearm, he looked Susie up and down and sideways. "It's the riot we're investigating now," he boomed in a deep voice. "Yesterday. You were there."

"My group didn't riot, but yes, I took part in the march."

"We need to talk to you about it."

"What's your name, Detective?"

"Bordick. James Bordick." His voice slipped into a higher register.

"I doubt I can help you, Detective Bordick, but please come in, both of you. It's much too hot out here."

Bordick clumped in first, glancing side to side and back toward the kitchen. Briefly Susie wondered what he made of her miscellaneous antique furniture, abstract prints, Mexican *retablos*, Hmong quilts, worn kilim rugs. Not that she cared.

The woman, Tate, took a seat on the sofa, following Susie's gesture, and Susie waited till Bordick also settled there before perching on a chair herself. Though she had nothing to hide (as she kept assuring herself, to keep herself calm), she wouldn't let police prowl uninvited.

Bordick set his hands on his knees expectantly. Tate took a pen and notepad from her pocket.

"Ms. Alioto," said Tate, "you're aware that fights and vandalism took place yesterday before the march broke up. A child was badly injured."

"I saw that in the paper, I'm sick about it, the poor little boy!" She saw no reason to conceal her feelings, and for clarity she continued: "You must realize that the groups organizing the march did not commit or encourage any vandalism. We do not condone it. And I was not, by the way, on the organizing committee, I'm no longer a leader in TeachPeace."

"Your sign was there, lady!" Bordick blurted. "With your slogan about kids' blood!"

As Susie took this in, Tate watched her for several long seconds before adding, "Your protest placard was discovered in the entryway of Gentle-Grounds, by the smashed window where the child was hurt."

Susie stared back at the detectives, anxiously tracing the links in her mind. So they had found her sign; then, most likely, they used photos of the event to spot who was carrying it; then a police officer identified her. Her name and face would be known to some of the local authorities.

Surveillance of mass gatherings was not unusual—despicable of course but not alarming. Yet she'd been ID'd with remarkable speed, given the crowd around her. *Wait, were the Philly cops now using facial recognition software for public events? Ohmigod. Creepy!*

She closed her mouth, which had hung open while she thought. She shouldn't appear taken aback. *Strong front*, she lectured herself, though her head felt woozy again.

"My sign," she managed to get out, "was *against* the spilling of kids' blood! My group has nothing to do with breaking windows."

Tate's eyes had locked on Susie. "You appeared to be hurt yourself," Tate continued, "when the glass broke. You were bleeding in the facial area. Was it that left ear you have bandaged? Then you spoke to one of the Black Bloc vandals, who assisted you in leaving the scene."

Now a chill ran along Susie's neck, and her shoulders hunched inadvertently. Surveillance with a vengeance—the Gestapo state in action! How many video cameras did they have? On the storefront and where else? What kind of technology analyzed the images? Susie's conviction that she had nothing to hide splintered like the window.

Bordick was glaring at her. Tate positioned her pen over the notepad and continued, "I hope you weren't badly injured, ma'am, and we have no reason at this time to believe you committed illegal acts yourself. Just give us the name of the Antifa that came to your aid."

Susie blinked several times. She sent a surreptitious "Don't Shake" order to her hands, her legs, her voice.

So far, the cops had shared information without extracting much from her. Let's keep it that way, she told herself. "I don't know who it was," she stated.

"Really?" Tate persisted. "A complete stranger stopped to help you?"

"Yeah.... I don't think, I don't think it was the same one that broke the glass."

"How do you know that?"

"Because of the way … the way he talked to me. He was … concerned."

"This Antifa was a male?"

"Mm, yeah. I thought so. Well, definitely."

When Bordick let out a skeptical snort, Susie added, "From his height. And his voice. His face was covered but the voice was a man's. A young man, sounded like."

Susie took a fraction of a second to commend herself for saying "young." It sounded honest, yet it was a fact they'd presume anyway.

"And where," Tate pursued, "did this individual take you?"

"Just to … a short distance—a block or two." How much had the cameras seen? "Till I was steady on my feet and clear of the commotion."

"He did not identify himself in any way?"

"No. In fact I don't know that he was Antifa. It could've been anybody dressed like—"

"Where did you go then?"

"Then? … I came home. I was dizzy. From the heat, and I was bleeding—like you said."

"How did you get home if you were dizzy?"

"The 48 bus. It runs a couple blocks from there, on Arch."

"Were the buses on their normal routes right after the demonstration?"

"Ahh … that one was. I don't know about others."

Tate jotted notes on her pad. Bordick leaned his head to the side, folded his arms, crossed his legs with one big foot—in an expensive-looking running shoe—against the wooden coffee table. His posture reinforced the cynicism in his scowl. Susie looked pointedly at the offending shoe, then stared him in the eye before speaking again to Tate in what she hoped was a plausible tone.

"Sorry I'm not much help. They do a good job of disguising themselves with those black hoods and masks."

After a few more minutes the interview ended when Tate handed Susie a card with contact information "in case you think of anything more. It's got my office number, mobile, email." On the way out, Tate gave Susie a stern appraising look while Bordick swaggered with his elbows splayed.

Retreating from the door, Susie sat down suddenly on the staircase, giving way to the shakes she'd been suppressing.

Had she slipped up by concealing too much? What could they pin on her?

She'd automatically followed her anarchist instincts, but now she questioned them. Why should she protect that Lauren girl anyway? Gratitude for dressing a wound didn't require getting herself in trouble by lying to the authorities. Birdbrain window-smashers didn't count as colleagues in the movement.

Gradually she forced her anxiety down. No problem here, no *problem*, she assured herself.

When she went to the kitchen for another dose of iced coffee, she exchanged a long look and a short conversation with the head of Errico on the refrigerator.

"To me a policeman is worse than a criminal," he reminded her.

"Right, that's why I didn't cooperate," she replied. "Still, if it gets me in trouble, I'll bust that Sean's head for him."

Errico smiled at that, and she went back to the living room to play a Folkways CD of her favorite music, antifascist songs from the Spanish Civil War, sung by Pete Seeger, Woody Guthrie and others. This should have calmed her nerves, but she found she was thinking back to that time, in her commune days, when she'd been guilty of more than concealment. Her heart raced.

When Eric slogged in an hour later, he winced as always at her music, and she turned down the volume before snapping at him: "Where were you? Did your shift run this late?"

He confessed he'd taken the opportunity to check out a Center City comic store, looking for the new issue of his favorite zine.

"How was the job then? Everything go well?"

"It was a job," he said, loping upstairs. "Basically."

He said no more about his day, nor did she mention the police visit.

8

It was Jenna Adelman with her hand up. No matter how much Susie tried to discourage traditional question-response methods in her classroom, these students were too well trained. Today, with the dozen seniors in her Honors American History course, she'd commandeered the school's Meeting Room, as she liked to do about once a month to facilitate free-ranging discussion. This was where the Board of Trustees met. Seated around the long mahogany table, the kids could make easy eye contact with each other, and they were not in the least intimidated by the rich wood or plush chairs. Still, at the beginning, they tended to raise their hands and wait for Susie to call on them.

"Yes, Jenna," she gestured from her seat among the students. "If no one else is talking, you can just speak up." Groggy from a poor night's sleep, Susie wanted the students to lead the discussion today for her sake as well as theirs.

"I think it's natural," Jenna said, "to get most upset when it's people you know that get killed. If it's somebody on the other side of the world, it's only, you know, kind of abstract."

In this swanky setting, Susie liked to pose topics that subtly undercut the workings of the capitalist state. Last week the class had studied the Vietnam War: the gradual escalations, the quandary of a U.S. military attempting to prop up a corrupt regime that had little popular support, the role of TV and other media in thrusting the conflict into people's living rooms, the maneuverings of politicians and the growth of antiwar protests. Today Susie had offered two points of view for the class to debate: (1) The rise and ultimate success of the antiwar movement proved the vigor of American democracy, the ability of the people to make their voice heard. (2) As long as the antiwar movement focused on the crimes and suffering in Southeast Asia, it remained marginal. Not until thousands of American soldiers returned home in body bags did the protests gain a wide audience. This showed that (a) Americans on the whole didn't care about abuses perpetrated by their government unless they themselves were directly affected, and (b) a modern state, even a so-called democracy, had great freedom to act without the actual consent of the governed.

To Susie these views were not mutually exclusive, but she was interested in whether her students would lean toward the optimistic or the pessimistic take. They were smart kids who'd benefited from their elite education at Hubble Day School, and most carried a certain smugness, a complacent belief in their ability to make their mark on the world. She tried to challenge that, and as a teacher who challenged, she was well respected at the school, even on occasion beloved.

Now Nick Carpinteria spoke up. Nick was a Community Scholar, one of the handful of Hubble Day students from a modest background, supported by a full scholarship. Gratefully, he did not raise his hand.

"Yeah," he said in response to Jenna, "I go along with that, but it's not just Americans. All over, people care about what's close to home. And you get behind your own whether they're right or not, which is, kind of, what they were saying with the pro-war slogans, 'America, Love It or Leave It,' 'My Country, Right or Wrong.' I mean it's maybe dumb, bigoted, whatever, but like Jenna said, it's natural."

"So it's natural for the public to be assholes," another student put in.

"Sure," still another picked up, "but if people organize—that was the point of the antiwar movement—if you rally together for a just cause, you can force politicos to do the right thing. In the long run the government has to respond to the people."

"Except … did the movement really make Nixon end the war? Remember the timeline. He kept up the bombing, pretended 'Vietnamization' was working, and real real slowly dropped American troop levels until he could sneak out the back door. Which is probably what he wanted to do all along."

"I don't think so. He would've gone on fighting forever if he didn't have to face the voters—because it was mostly poor kids getting killed, minorities."

"Isn't that an exaggeration? About the minorities? 'Cause the draft was still on, till '73, so middle-class kids got pulled in too. You and me, we coulda been drafted."

The debate went on, with minor guidance from Susie, and she was impressed with the students' grasp of the material and willingness to engage with complicated questions. Overall they seemed cynical about human nature and politicians but hopeful about democracy—an interesting and perhaps contradictory position, one that she often shared despite her theoretical commitment to abolishing the state.

After the class, during a free period, she headed back to her own classroom. Instead of feeling energized by the discussion, she hunched at her desk with her head in her hands. All night she'd fidgeted in bed, beset by images of little Matty in his hospital bed, students bleeding to death from gunfire in hallways, black-clad figures shattering glass amid incomprehensible blasts from megaphones, Matty's uncle gazing at her suspiciously, cops spying through surveillance cameras, NRA fat cats writing checks to congressmen.… In one dream she saw herself being arrested, charged with gouging out someone's eye. *I didn't do it*, she yelled from a padded cell with no windows. *Not this time.* The walls began to squeeze in on her, trapping her legs so she couldn't move; her arms too were paralyzed ... until she woke with the sheets wrapped tight and both fists clenched against her neck.

Now, in her classroom, a cloud of apprehension persisted. Maybe another cup of coffee would help, though she had no appetite for food or drink.

While she debated going to the teachers' lounge, muted notes sounded from the bottom desk drawer—the little red phone stuffed in her handbag. She couldn't fish it out in time to answer, and when she saw the caller's number she didn't recognize it. A minute later, the phone signaled a voicemail.

Dialing in, she heard the crackly tones of that girl.

"Ms. Alioto, hi, this is Lauren. From the other day. Just wondering if you're okay. I mean, we didn't do a concussion test or anything, I started worrying about that. You were unconscious a minute or two at least, so have you had a headache or, like, vision problems? 'Cause if you have, you should be evaluated. And the ear, is it healing up without stitches? Call back or, like, text me if there's problems because we, like I said, I mean, I'm sure who*ever* was involved, they didn't want to, you know what I mean."

No, Susie wanted to snap, I don't know what you mean when you hedge like that, but if you're admitting some responsibility for the imbecilic actions at the march, I'll take it. She poised her finger to delete the message, then changed her mind.

Anger at Lauren perked her up, and she got through the rest of her classes without dragging. At home later, she discovered Eric asleep upstairs after his shift at the coffee shop. She tiptoed back down to the living room so as not to disturb him. Debating whether to respond to Lauren, she listened to the message again. Not only was the evasiveness annoying, but the girl betrayed no knowledge that a child had been injured. Was it possible she hadn't heard? Probably she ignored traditional news outlets, but wouldn't the story have splashed across social media? Eric wasn't around to ask, and it seemed outrageous that reckless window smashers might avoid knowing the consequences of their behavior.

In essence, for Susie, this became a teachable moment. Her thumb found the option to return the call. When Lauren answered, she launched right in.

"This is Susie Alioto. Did you hear about Matty Gutierrez?"

"Who?"

"The little boy in the coffee shop whose face got sliced up by the falling glass."

"Oh, him. Yeah, the kid."

"And do you still support the use of random, uncoordinated violence that serves no strategic purpose?"

"It wasn't random! … I mean, whoever did it, that whole area around City Hall, it's banks and investment thieves, lawyers—the super-rich sucking up to the politicals. Any strike there is justified."

"Think about it a minute, Lauren. Children don't deserve protection? Our march was about saving children from guns!"

"The kid shouldn't've been there. He had no business being there!"

"Four years old—how was he to know that?"

"I mean … his parents, his nanny, whoever's in charge of him."

"His mother had nobody else to look after him on a Sunday. I believe, reading between the lines of the news story, she's a single mother."

"Maybe, I don't know…. Anyway, there's bound to be some, you know, collateral damage. In any direct action."

"Lauren, really? 'Collateral damage'? You use dehumanizing language from the military?"

"It's a military-type fight, isn't it? They use clubs and tasers and guns and gas on us, we fight back."

"There weren't any tasers or guns yesterday," Susie snorted. "Listen, Lauren. Do you know what Federica Montseny said about being accountable? She said we must 'create in each person a sense of responsibility in order that each one of us can have the right to enjoy all his rights.' In other words, the revolution won't work until everyone owns their actions."

"Who the fuck," muttered Lauren, "is Faydreeka Moan Sane?"

"Someone you should read. Listen, if you won't accept moral responsibility, at least be aware of the possible legal consequences. The police have already come after me. They showed up at my door yesterday, asked what I knew about the person that helped me on the sidewalk."

"*What?*"

"Modern surveillance techniques, kid. You should know what you're up against."

"*Fuck fuck fuck.* What'd you tell them?"

"Nothing about you. I said I didn't know who was behind the mask. On the other hand, if they're tapping my phone now …"

"Ohmigod!"

Susie chuckled to herself. Stoking the girl's paranoia—this was fun. After a beat, she added, "Relax, I don't think they're listening. We still have *some* constitutional protections…. But if you're planning more attacks, do consider the practical implications."

"We don't share plans with outsiders."

"I didn't say you should. Just show some common sense, please."

"You have no—no right to lecture me! *I'm* the one that helped *you*. Not that a person should be *grateful* or anything."

Susie sighed. "Ye-eah, you're right. It's just that you're so …" She started to say "naïve" but changed the word to "young."

That hung in the air a moment, with no response from Lauren, who probably found it insulting. As Susie herself would have, she realized, when she was Lauren's age.

"By the way," Susie added, "my ear is improving, and I don't have a concussion. Thanks for your concern."

"Good," said Lauren, and hung up.

9

Eric woke with a headache. Having come straight home when his shift ended, he'd collapsed into bed and slept for two and a half hours. After his training session yesterday, Monday, he'd been assigned the morning shift for the rest of the week, 6 a.m. to 1:30 p.m., meaning he had to leave the house by 5:20, an ungodly hour, even earlier than his mother the teacher. And then he'd been on his feet for seven hours straight with few breaks. First the commuters, then the nanny coffee klatch with toddlers from Center City's high-rises, then the writer/artist/loafer types who sat at the clustered tables and studiously managed not to look at each other, then the lunch rush—no time to grab a snack or latte for himself. His previous job at the coffee shop near campus had been less busy, less stressful; now he thought he understood what was meant by exploitation of the working class.

Also, his coworker Melinda had behaved snottily today, answering his questions with an ironic lilt. Shit, after a few hours of training, did they expect him to know every one of the store's procedures? How was he supposed to tell an apple walnut muffin from a banana nut when they were wrapped in plastic and not labeled? Even the amazing way Melinda filled out her black T-shirt didn't excuse her obnoxiousness. And the boss, Mr. Sambucco, mostly hung out in back with his phone to his ear, barking phrases like "zoning variance" and "facade inspection," which to Eric did not smack of good management.

Now, with his head pounding after his nap, he wondered whether he'd have to force new settings on his circadian clock, which normally slotted on-line role-playing games at 2:30 a.m. He resented the pressure to change his lifestyle. All through college he'd worked 10–15 hours a week to supplement his scholarship money and keep student loans to a minimum, but none of his jobs had involved rising before daylight.

When he stumbled to the bathroom for a giant piss, the mirror confirmed that he looked as wiped out as he felt. He thought about combing his hair with his fingers, or at least flattening it, but that required too much effort.

He thumped downstairs, where he found Susie slumped on the sofa listening to her Spanish Civil War music again, simpleminded lyrics set to childish tunes with twangy banjos and uninspired guitars. Personally, Eric hoped that if the government ever managed an effective ban on assault weapons, banjos would be included. But he contained himself and uttered only one word to his mother: "Dinner?"

A word that could suggest, he later argued to himself, "Do you have any plans for dinner? Shall I arrange something for us both?" From her glower, though, it was clear that she mistook his innocent question to mean, "When are you making dinner for me?"—a task that (a) she had explicitly explained he should not expect from her this summer and (b) she had nevertheless performed most nights since he moved home.

Eric felt he appreciated women's rights in general and, in particular, his mother's refusal to serve as a cook for a grown man. Which did not mean he wanted to be a cook himself. Yet he felt he'd outgrown the life stage of pizza every night and cold pizza for breakfast. At the same time, a quick mental calculation of his pay after deductions told him he couldn't afford high-class takeout. It was a quandary.

Luckily he was spared an immediate scolding for his faux pas because, as his mother scowled and opened her mouth to blast him, her red cell phone rang. Uncharacteristically, it was sitting within easy reach. She held up a finger to tell him to stay put while she lowered the music and answered the call.

Veering into an estimate of the volume of tips needed to make a significant difference in the affordability of fish tacos, Eric missed the beginning of the phone conversation. He woke to attention again at the phrase "little Matty."

"That's *such* good news," his mother went on. "Do they think he'll get 100 percent of his sight back? ... Oh, of course, yeah, it'll take a while.... Right.... Joe, thank you so much for keeping me up to date. I had trouble sleeping last night, worrying about the boy."

Joe? Trouble sleeping?

In a moment Eric guessed the caller's identity. That was a surprise, as was his mother's worry about a little kid she'd never met. Had she really lain awake last night? She hadn't mentioned that to him; on the other hand, she was too principled to lie about it.

"Yes, sure, do keep me posted," Susie said warmly, cuddling the phone against her unwounded ear. "And do you think, would Rita appreciate a note from me? If you tell her who I am?"

It always startled him, the depth of Susie's feelings for miscellaneous people who were oppressed, in pain, persecuted, whatever. He himself was not so easily affected, and he considered it impractical and unrealistic to go around grieving for the suffering in the world. There was just too much of it, with too little hope of remedy. Yet it did move him, in a way he didn't quite understand, to see how quick and hot his mother's empathy ran. He was secretly proud of her for being that kind of person.

She motioned for Eric to bring her pencil and paper. He fetched them from the kitchen, and she scribbled something on the pad.

"Got it. Thank you, Joe," she bubbled. "Yes, do, please."

After she hung up, staring at her lap, it took a moment for her to notice Eric again. "Guess what?" she chirped up at him. "The little boy, Matty? His second surgery went well, and there's a good chance his eye will recover. At least mostly. He'll have scars though."

"Wonderful," said Eric. And with a careful smile, he retreated upstairs before she remembered to scold him about making his own dinner.

10

To Susie, it seemed like a good idea to take her friend Margaret to GentleGrounds for a snack after the movie matinee on Saturday. Too disciplined to succumb to theater popcorn or candy, both women were starved, and Margaret was eager to talk about the film, so they tramped the mile and a half to the coffee shop. Thankfully the month had decided to behave like May again, with balmy afternoon weather.

A tall and wide, large-boned woman only a year younger than Susie, Margaret was huffing by the time they entered the store. "We've hiked for half an hour," she grumped. "What's so special about—"

"This is the place whose window was broken during the march. Where the little boy got hurt and my ear was nicked. I feel like we ought to support them."

"Oh. The window looks fine now."

"They've fixed it. Look, they *do* have them today—cream-filled brownie cookies! I saw a picture online."

Margaret bent to peer into the display case. "For you maybe. For me, even a picture of those things has too many calories."

Margaret settled for a plain bagel with red pepper hummus while Susie indulged in the brownie treat with added whipped cream on top. Both asked for iced coffee, and they took their cups plus a chrome stand with their order number to a corner table.

"This place is the ultra in ultramodern," Margaret observed, checking out the glass/metal/fiberglass ambience. "I feel like I'm not dressed for it." Actually Margaret's black slacks and maroon turtleneck tunic were considerably more elegant than Susie's jeans and gingham top, but Susie let the comment go. Margaret also colored her hair and wore makeup, enhancements that Susie never allowed herself. And for Margaret, Susie couldn't help but notice, they worked; she looked no more than 50.

"Well, I found that movie depressing," Susie said. "Two really old and really sick people on their last trip together—who wants to see that?"

Remembering that Margaret had lost her husband a few years ago to cancer—one of the diseases in the film—Susie had an instant of regret, but Margaret didn't take the story personally.

"Ooh—this coffee is strong!" Margaret said. "… But it was honest, and cute, don't you think? And kind of charming, too, the way they reminisced together, each reminding the other of things they'd forgotten."

"Then it ends in murder-suicide because their illnesses are too much to bear? That's not charming. Maybe not even honest. I need this coffee to scour it out of my brain!"

Margaret winced. "It was well acted, at least," she offered. "I do love everything Dame Alice does."

"Me too, usually. But she deserved a better script. With a different ending."

"We'll agree to disagree then," Margaret smiled, always more willing to compromise than Susie. A retired third-grade public school teacher, she had decades of experience in resolving differences.

Their food arrived suddenly, by way of a hairy forearm accompanied by a booming voice. "Good afternoon, Susie!"

"Oh." She looked up, startled. "Oh, hi, Mr. Sambu—"

"Joe, please. Just plain Joe." His bald head perspired despite the shop's cool atmosphere. Today, over his business slacks and white dress shirt with rolled sleeves, he wore a black apron with the GentleGrounds logo in white. "It's so good to see you. And I have to tell you, you're gonna like this brownie cookie, it's the all-time best. Rita's own recipe."

"It looks lovely."

"Speaking of which, who is your lovely companion today?"

"Ah. This is my friend Margaret Pasicznyk. We've just come from a matinee. It was a long dull movie and we're famished."

Joe reached across the table to shake Margaret's hand. "Pleased to meet you. Is there anything I can get you for your bagel? Some lettuce and tomato? Onion?"

Margaret shook her head, visibly nonplussed by what she took to be an overly chummy waiter.

Turning back to Susie, Joe said, "Looks like your ear healed up good. Happy to see that."

"Thanks." Self-consciously Susie fingered her ear, which she knew was still purplish. "Joe's part owner of this store," Susie clarified for Margaret. "Actually the whole chain of GentleGrounds stores. It was his niece Rita's little boy whose face and eye were cut. Little Matty had to have surgery at Children's— Joe, how's his recovery?"

"Real good. He's home now, and they still think his vision may turn out okay. The scars on his face, maybe they'll deal with that later."

"I'm so glad he's out of the hospital."

"It's awful that anyone was hurt," said Margaret. "I was way in the back on the other side of the street, and when people started running I couldn't tell what was going on."

"Margaret's also a member of TeachPeace," Susie explained.

"Ah!" Joe locked eyes with Margaret. "Did you see the thugs? The ones that busted stuff?"

"No. It must've been just a few of them. Where I was, we had no idea ..."

"Sorry," Joe apologized. "Don't mean to put you on the spot. I know it wasn't you people that went crazy.... But don't let me interrupt you, ladies. Thank you for stopping in, and please enjoy your snack. Susie, I'll keep you up to date on Matty's progress like I promised."

After he disappeared behind the counter, Susie took a sip of iced coffee and contemplated whether to attack the brownie with fingers or a fork.

Margaret exhaled. "Hmm," she murmured, and after a few seconds: "How do you know him?"

"Oh, didn't I tell you? Eric's working here now."

"Eric?"

"Yeah, he's off today, probably still asleep.... When I heard little Matty was hurt, I came in to tell the managers how bad we felt about it. Because the public statement Miriam put out—it was, I don't know, generic, and I felt we ought to say something personal. Though really I was speaking for myself, not TeachPeace."

"That's so like you, Susie."

"It's the least we could do."

Both women dug into their food. Susie's brownie-cookie-cream was, as predicted, scrumptious—her most decadent treat in months.

"That Joe seems like a nice guy," Margaret said after a couple of minutes, between chews. "And he's taking an interest in you."

"Interest?" Susie laughed. "Being friendly?"

"Seems a little more than friendly." Margaret pursed her lips. "But why," she added, "would he suggest putting lettuce on a bagel? Doesn't he know that some things don't belong together?"

"You're such a bigot," Susie countered. "I put lettuce on bagels. Peanut butter too."

"Ugh! Please, confine your anarchism to politics."

* * *

Taking an "interest" in her? At the kitchen table that evening, trying to finalize her lesson plans for Monday, Susie struggled to concentrate.

By the time she and Margaret left the coffee shop, the scene had felt odd to her. They were the oldest people in the place, definitely not the typical customers, and yet Joe had continued to give them special attention, offering refills of their iced coffee and waving as they left.

Now, when she pictured him hovering over the table, his face, general build and hairless crown reminded her of her old landlord, Mr. Papadopoulos, the man who'd owned the commune building. The connection made her snicker, but for the rest of the night her mind drifted through seemingly random images and her lesson plans went nowhere.

11

Back in 1976 it was the cheapest place available, the ramshackle three-story row house in West Philly with an ancient furnace, drafty windows and wobbly banisters, not to mention the hole in the kitchen wall where a scurry of little feet could be heard. But it was close to other anarchist communes and the food coop where they all took shifts. With eight young people pooling resources, sometimes even sharing clothes, they could devote themselves to the cause.

Susie moved in right after college. Though she was grateful to her parents—a lawyer and a United Way exec—for financing her four years at a fine liberal arts school, there was no way she'd return to their green-leafed, all-light-complexioned suburb. As an undergraduate she'd read books on anarchist and communist theory and devoted her senior honors thesis to the ideas and influence of Malatesta. She'd taken part in campus protests deploring the later stages of the Vietnam War, supporting the Equal Rights Amendment, condemning the authorities for the shootout at the Pine Ridge Indian Reservation. She'd gotten trashed with friends to celebrate the resignation of President Nixon. By graduation she considered herself ready for serious, adult activism.

She plunged right into the commune's work: helping at the food coop, collecting books for prisoners, running discussion forums, organizing demonstrations and street theater. The other members became her best friends, almost her only friends, since there was little time or money for recreation. Soon she parlayed her honors degree into a teaching job at an alternative school—open classrooms, fluid grade levels, disdain for textbooks—and though her salary was paltry by bourgeois standards, it became a mainstay for the commune.

Now, when she thought back to that time, she pictured first of all the labor—sorting and packing stacks of books; opening a chilly deserted storefront to set up folding chairs for a debate on a subject she could no longer remember; tending a huge, stained, steaming pot of chicken stock that spread a thick smell of bird carcass and miscellaneous vegetable fragments; sewing a patch on top of a patch on jeans that had worn out long ago.

When Susie's parents came into town, she met them at a restaurant or other neutral place, in the best clothes she could find. She knew they wouldn't understand why her friends went around the house in shabby coats and fingerless knit gloves instead of turning up the heat (which didn't work well anyway) or why the carpetless living room was occupied by batches of poster board, cans of paint, heaps of leaflets and newsletters. And she certainly didn't want them to suppose she ought to be rescued from this environment.

The only older person who entered the house, as far as Susie remembered, was the middle-aged landlord, Papadopoulos. They had to summon him when the furnace or stove broke down or when the splintery back door refused to shut. Nothing he did solved the problems, but Papa Dump, as they called him, seemed to like showing up and chatting. In the summer, when a couple of the women didn't bother with bras under their T-shirts, he was especially eager to hang around.

They would laugh about him afterward. He must have thought that anarchism meant free love, which it did, in a way, in the sense of being free to love whomever you wanted however you wanted. But they took their relationships seriously, because sexual jealousy or recrimination would disrupt the mission. If a pair broke up, an unwritten rule said at least one of the two should leave the house.

Over time, as Susie became the longest-tenured member, she shared a bed with three others, none for less than three years, and the end of the last of these unions, with Greg, prompted her exit from the commune.

By the time of that crisis, Susie had left her youth behind amid the discarded posters and outdated manifestos. During almost 18 years in the house she'd written hundreds of handouts and press releases, cooked a thousand pots of broth, and watched as the original crew drifted away into mainstream organizations or graduate school. Increasingly she had to act the role of mother to the younger members, reminding them to clean the bathroom or put away laundry. Being a mother without motherhood was not much fun, and she felt her experience was often ignored and her tolerance abused. Worse, though the pressing political issues had evolved over the years, the goal of a just, compassionate society seemed as far away as ever.

That December when she turned 40, Greg Mueller was only 27, still impulsive and cocksure of himself, and since she'd invited him into the house four years before, he'd shown less and less willingness to listen to communal reason. That month the group was concentrating on President Clinton's weakling "Don't Ask, Don't Tell" compromise on gays in the military; three separate protests had slammed this Christmas gift to gay rights as nothing but a cheat. Early in the new year, Greg wanted to change the focus to support the Zapatistas rebelling against the Mexican government and the North American Free Trade Agreement. Everyone else in the house wanted to stick with gay rights, but Greg insisted that sinister U.S.-backed neoliberalism demanded action. His demand led to a small gathering in icy weather outside a Latino church in North Philly, where most of the residents stared as if the protesters were insane cultists, especially after the street theater enactment of a scene from the news:

Mayan rebels shot in the back of the head in the market of Ocosingo.

When a frozen Susie returned to the house at 3:00, tired and starved because she'd missed lunch, she found Papa Dump, balder and fatter than in earlier years, making himself at home with a sandwich in the kitchen. "Who let you in?" she yelled. "Are you eating our food? What's going on here?" Though he claimed to be bleeding the radiators, she blew her top and chased him out. When others criticized her for impeding maintenance on the house, she snapped back, pointing out that he never fixed anything right himself and never paid for a competent handyman. By evening her ill temper led to a breakup with Greg, whom she told that his impersonation of a Mayan corpse was the stupidest thing she'd ever seen.

She found a tiny apartment in Center City and declared, to herself, that it was time for a new life with new, grownup friends. Soon she met an interesting neighbor, Margie Pasicznyk, also a teacher, and they became buddies. By the next school year she'd left the low-paying alternative school in West Philly for the highly respected Hubble Day School, which offered health insurance and other benefits. After three years there, she scraped together the down payment for a small house in the Fairmount section.

She wasn't abandoning her beliefs or her activism, she told herself, and proved it by purchasing the Malatesta poster at an anarchist bookstore and giving it a prominent place on her refrigerator.

Soon after that, however, when she found herself accidentally pregnant, she had to wonder whether she'd grown up at all.

12

After the disagreeable movie and the snack at GentleGrounds, Susie slept fitfully that night. For years she'd occasionally had a recurring dream set in the commune, where she hovered over the stock pot, stirring and stirring. Around her, cheerful voices surged and waned, and sometimes a friendly hand massaged her weary shoulders; but when she turned to look, she didn't always recognize the faces—new people had sneaked in somehow, it wasn't clear when, and they made her uneasy, she didn't know why, and all the while her job was to keep stirring and stirring and stirring, for if she stopped something bad would happen.

Tonight the dream returned, altered in a strange way. Papa Dump was there, leering at her, and not only his face but the others circling around had grown old and distorted. Then one young person appeared—who? Oh, it was the Antifa girl, what's-her-name. "We're *not* Antifa," she chided Susie, and then smashed the kitchen windows with a saucepan. Some of the others applauded and cheered, shouting about propaganda of the deed, but Susie shivered in the chill wind streaming through the broken glass. Papa Dump wanted to rub her goose-bumped arms, but she thrust him away. Then, sailing in on the breeze came Marty Leffler with his clarinet, and as he played a long riff, Susie knew she was going to sleep with him and get pregnant. When he put his hands on her waist, she tried to run but didn't really want to run, and her feet refused to move.

She woke up in a cold sweat, with the covers kicked off and her face turned to the chugging air conditioner. Staggering out of bed, she switched off the unit and clomped to the toilet. In the sudden glare of the bathroom light, the little old lady stared from the mirror.

II

If William Penn, in his bronze incarnation on City Hall, had rotated 84 degrees to the right, he might have peered down on a sunny block lined with old three-story brick and stucco buildings that had survived the ongoing transition to apartment towers and condos. The ground level featured a variety of shops: small grocery, used bookstore, hairdresser, Indian restaurant. At the end of the row, outdoor tables topped with colorful umbrellas flanked the corner. It was a scene Penn might have admired: a cheerful late-May morning with the city and its people in apparent harmony.

13

Susie sat at a sidewalk table, under a bright blue umbrella, enjoying her brunch of avocado halves stuffed with scrambled eggs, black beans, spicy ground beef and queso sauce. Though the dish's name, the Black Widow Special, lacked diplomacy, she'd opted for adventure. When the heaping plate appeared before her, she grimaced at the size of it but then smirked at her companion, who was confronted by a colossal mound of French toast made of challah bread and stuffed with cream cheese and bananas, topped with other fruit in a display grand enough to qualify as sculpture.

"*Meglio poco che niente*,' my dear nonna used to say."

"Yes?" Susie asked.

"What, you don't speaka the mother tongue?"

"Not much, sorry," smiled Susie, aiming her fork at an outcropping of egg.

"'Better little than nothing.' Which is what she had, a little. Never in her life a breakfast like this."

"Well, I could use her help with mine. And a few of her brothers and sisters, if she had any."

"Two sisters," Joe confirmed. "Parents brought 'em over after the Great War."

"My Italian forbears immigrated about a generation earlier, and by the time I came along there wasn't much Umbria left in them. I've always wished I were more ethnic, but my grandma got her spaghetti sauce out of a jar."

"Ugh! Sacrilege! Mine brought all their traditions. I think they were just escaping the Mussolini fascist crap."

"That's smart of them. And I'm glad you're not one of those people who say, 'At least Mussolini made the trains run on time.' Which is actually untrue. Fake news."

"My people were too poor to ride trains. They begged and borrowed to pay for steerage. Got jammed in the ship's hold with hundreds of others."

"Economic injustice," Susie added after a sip of iced coffee, "that's at the heart of so many of our problems, maybe all of them. The swindling tax plan that … Oh, sorry, I didn't mean to go off on politics."

Susie was having too good a time to risk offending this decent man who'd invited her to her first brunch in the past decade. Restaurant brunches— a custom of the privileged classes, she thought. Even if she could afford them now and then, she considered herself too busy with important matters to waste time on a nouveau capitalist extravagance. Last year, when Eric suggested a brunch on Mother's Day, she'd laughed at him. This year he'd merely dropped a store-bought card on the kitchen table and kissed the top of her head. So why had she accepted Joe's invite?—she didn't know, and at the moment didn't care.

Though Joe had offered to pick her up, Susie had taken a bus. She'd dressed as she would for school, namely, a nice yellow blouse and tan slacks. Her appetite had rebounded enough for her to savor every chunk of avocado and each bite of peppery beef.

After soaking his mass of French toast in maple syrup, Joe was digging in like an old-time railroad man shoveling coal into the boiler. This mental image amused Susie, and she smiled at him.

"You can talk politics if you want," he paused to dab his broad lips with a napkin, "I don't mind. I may not agree with you, I don't do protests and that kinda thing. But, y'know, people wanting to get ahead, make a place for themselves, I'm all for that. Which is why I went in with Rita."

Susie had already heard the latest update on Rita's son, who continued to recover from the surgeries. And Joe knew she'd sent Rita a personal note of sympathy and encouragement.

Susie said, "I'm sure Rita's grateful for your help while she stays with Matty. And for all you've done as her—what did you call it?—her financial person."

"Yeah, financial. She needed that kinda help, getting the business off the ground."

"For a young entrepreneur, that's understandable."

He leaned forward and lowered his voice. "What I mean, there was another thing. Just when she's graduating from that cooking school, turns out she's pregnant. I love the girl, but that's not smart. The guy was a total loser, but she wouldn't give up the kid. Which I don't blame her, I'm glad she didn't."

"Oh.… With a baby, yes, I know, it's much harder.… So is he, I mean Matty's father, is he still with her?"

"Hell no."

"I … ," Susie said, dropping her eyes to her plate, "can sympathize."

"Yeah, thanks. Kind of typical, huh? The way it is today."

"Actually … just after Eric was born, I was in a similar situation.… His father ran off with a clarinet."

"He what?"

"Never mind. Long story." Susie filled her mouth with egg, discomfited by her confession. Joe hadn't asked her marital status; why did she need to tell him? For that matter, she hadn't asked his. He didn't wear a ring, but that didn't mean anything.

Joe slurped his coffee, forked another wad of French toast, gave it a minimal chew and swallowed. "See, Rita's such a smart girl, I couldn't let her fall on her face. She had this idea for coffee shops, how to make 'em more attractive, draw the public. I mean, to me, coffee's coffee, like this cup here's pretty good, I don't know. But she had this inspiration, but then she had the kid, debt from cooking school, no resources.... Because my sister Tina," he paused to clear his throat, "that's Rita's mom, she picked a, well, kind of a loser-type too. Which I don't mean in a bad way. My brother-in-law, Mike Gutierrez, Tina met him in Colombia and that's where they lived when Rita was a kid. Mike's a nice guy but he doesn't earn much, they're just scraping by, so I figure I'm the one that's got to look after the family. There's three younger ones after Rita, they'll need help with college, whatever they need to do to get started in life."

Struggling to absorb this information, Susie murmured, "You're planning to help all of your nieces and nephews? That sounds like a lot of responsibility."

Joe shrugged. "Like I said, they're family. My nonna would get it—100 percent."

"I imagine she would. So … Joe, do you have any children of your own?"

"Nope." He frowned at his fork. "Never found the right momma for them, I guess."

"That's a shame. I think you'd make a good father."

"Maybe," he allowed, and then grinned. "But it's easier being the rich uncle. Never had to change diapers, don't have to yell about curfews."

With a surprisingly delicate motion of his big mitt, Joe signaled the waitress to refill his cup. "You need more ice coffee?" he asked Susie. "Anything?"

"A larger stomach."

"Ah, you can do it, lady, tuck in, tuck in."

Susie noticed that Joe's plate was already two-thirds empty while hers remained nearly full. With a deep sigh, taking a respite from the monument of eggs, beef and beans, she turned halfway around to scan the sunny street and sidewalk. The air smelled of early roses, coffee and syrup. Lots of people were out, many with dogs or babies or both, the dogs sniffing eagerly toward the tables, the babies poking their toes out from expensive canopied strollers. When she started to turn back to Joe, something in the corner of her vision caused a doubletake.

The young woman, approaching from behind Susie, first glanced away, then seemed to reconcile herself to the contact. The young man, after one sharp squint, gazed off in the distance.

"Lauren," Susie called. "Hi, how are you?"

"Okay," said the girl, pausing with apparent reluctance by the table.

"Hi," Susie went on to Sean, "nice to see you. But I thought you didn't like bougie neighborhoods," she joked.

The skinny Sean had an odd way of standing, like an italic exclamation point, straight but tilted away as if he didn't want to be part of this scene. He left the response to Lauren, who said, "We're just out for a walk. Um, exercise? But I've heard of this place, it's, like, famous for breakfast, right?"

"Absolutely," Susie said. Indicating her plate, she added, "Look at the size of what you get."

"Uh, what exactly *is* that?"

"It's called the Black Widow Special. Spicy. I think it has everything in it except spiders.... Look, my ear healed up well. It may not be pretty, but thanks to your first aid …"

"No problem."

At this point Susie noticed that Sean had abandoned his pose of indifference in order to stare at Joe, who was returning the gaze with his mouth set in a line.

"I'm sorry, I forgot, this is my friend Joe. Joe, Lauren and Sean."

Lauren nodded with a muted "hi." Joe grunted. Sean merely blinked.

The waitress interrupted with the coffee pot. When she left, Joe sat with both palms flat on the table as if waiting for something else.

"Okay," Lauren muttered, "it's nice to see you."

"Right. Enjoy your walk."

After watching the two turn the corner, Joe kept quiet for a couple of minutes, taking two large bites of his French toast, gulping more coffee.

"So," he finally said, "that girl, she did first aid on your ear? Like after the riot?"

With a small sarcastic huff, Susie said, "Remember, Joe, the march wasn't a riot. Despite what happened to your window."

"Yeah, yeah. You know her good?"

"Lauren? … No, I met her just that day. She's in nursing school, she offered help."

"Because I seen her boyfriend before."

"You have?"

"Pretty sure. What's his last name?"

"I don't know."

"They were part of your demonstrator crowd?"

It suddenly struck Susie that she'd introduced Joe to the guy who had probably broken his window and injured his nephew. Where was her brain? Joe was no threat, but she ought to be more prudent.

"Uh … Lauren came up to me after I was hurt. On my way to the bus. I guess they both had been marching, I hadn't seen them before that. How do *you* know him?"

"I *don't* know him. Never mind."

Susie resumed working on her brunch, and eventually Joe came to her assistance by offloading some of the Black Widow onto his plate.

When they finished, he picked up the check in spite of her protest. "My treat. Because you sent that real nice card to my Rita."

"Which cost me a postage stamp. You don't need to repay me."

"Shush, shhh. My pleasure." His credit card slid easily from his wallet, and the waitress materialized to process it.

When Susie rose from the table, she needed an instant to find her balance with the extra weight in her stomach.

"So when," Joe said as he stood, his chair rasping against the pavement. "No, put it like this: Would you mind a whole lot if I call you again?"

"Mind?"

"Like, maybe dinner next time?"

What? Susie thought.

Had he assumed this was a *date*?

And yet she knew her thoughts had headed that way as well, as improbable as it might seem.

The sun over the sidewalk grew very bright, stark almost, as she straightened her collar, pleased she had worn her good yellow blouse.

"Of course not. I mean, I don't mind at all."

14

Eric professed to have no opinion about his mother's romantic life. Even when he was younger, he'd tried to stay neutral, as long as the guy wasn't pretending to advise him about video games or music. If a male friend of Susie's had wanted to move into the house and assert TV rights, that might have been different, but none came close to that.

There hadn't been many overall, and those he met or heard about didn't linger long. Julio was the exception—the young science teacher with whom Susie had caused much gossip in the corridors of Hubble Day School. It had been touchy enough for Eric to attend a school where his mother taught; but when the rumors flew that Ms. Alioto was dating a faculty member 28 years her junior, it became excruciating. But then Julio left to resume graduate work—this was, what, eight years ago now—and things returned to normal. Normal being Susie more interested in dead anarchists than in living males.

Ever since Eric could remember, she'd had that ancient Malatesta poster on the side of the refrigerator. He was a weird dude to reverence, so funny-looking in that photo: bizarre hair, loony eyes, a jutting beard, and was that a hint of an ironic smile? And his quote about the impossible being possible?— totally illogical. In his own life, judging from what Eric had read about him, this anarchist crank had been ridiculously ineffectual. So much scampering from place to place to avoid the authorities!—escaping in a large box of sewing machines, for instance, or being smuggled out of England in a coal boat. The one time Malatesta helped organize an actual armed rebellion, in southern Italy, the gang of insurrectionists got defeated in a few days, mostly by rain, snow and hunger, which kind of indicated a deficit in planning, right?

When Eric was nine, Susie had splurged on a trip to Italy for the two of them, and there, besides touring dull museums and churches, they'd visited the little towns where Malatesta's rebels had invaded municipal buildings and torched official documents. Of course the area was totally different now, but still it felt absurd to sit outside a café and snack on *tartelletta con crema soffice* while contemplating farcical attempts to free the people by burning papers. At that point the young Eric needed no further convincing that he should keep as far away as possible from his mother's nutty passions.

In the past few years Susie had mentioned Malatesta more often than any living male friends. Now, though, this guy Joe Sambucco was making inroads. She'd gone out with him three times in two weeks, and despite Eric's desire to remain aloof, Susie's dating his boss created an awkwardness.

When Susie asked him how things were going at the coffee shop, he couldn't say frankly that he hated it. (Balky "high-end" espresso machines, indecisive customers, expensive strollers blocking the aisles, snotty Melinda's lack of appreciation for his latte-making talents ...) And when Joe asked if his mother had gotten over her sniffles, he couldn't say, "What sniffles?"

The situation would resolve soon enough, since Eric would leave for Seattle by mid-August. But that prospect was making him uneasy in a couple of respects. First, the more he read about the professor he most hoped to work with, Nasrin Sassani, a prominent specialist in non-abelian groups, the more nervous he became that he wouldn't measure up. Mathematics had always come intuitively for him, but she was known for demanding rigorous formal logic; recently she'd gained public notoriety by finding a flaw in a paper that purported to prove, at long last, a centuries-old conjecture. Maybe she'd find big holes in Eric's thinking as well. In the few emails he'd already exchanged with her, she came off as severe, with a focus on "requirements" and "preparation."

A second reason for uneasiness was his newfound worry about his mother. Now that she suddenly seemed vulnerable to him—older, grayer, no longer the indomitable force she'd always appeared to be—he worried about leaving her alone when he moved out West. Yes, she'd lived alone the past four years, but as an undergrad he'd been only 40 minutes away.

For the time being at least, he wanted to "keep an eye on her," as he put it to himself. He didn't want her to get emotionally hurt again, for one thing. He knew Julio had been a big blow, though Susie would never admit it. (Actually, losing Julio was also sad for Eric, who liked the guy and thought his scientific mind a nice balance for his mom's political fantasies.) As for this Joe Sambucco—he was definitely an odd type for Susie, not college educated, not intellectual, not radical, just ... boring.

Watching over his mother caused a certain embarrassment. He wouldn't want her watching over *his* relationships, would he? Admittedly that was a moot point at the moment, his one college semi-girlfriend having moved to Chicago and Melinda being so fucking standoffish. Still ...

In any case, the "keeping an eye" consisted at first only of noting when Susie met up with Joe and what time she returned to the house. Plus, Eric continued to postpone an act he'd once been determined to accomplish when he came of age: changing his middle name. For the past year he'd been contemplating options but hadn't found an appropriate choice that would retain his initials, and his college friends proved unhelpful, suggesting alternatives like Mathnerd, Moonbeam, Microbrew and (from a history major) Mugwump. Lately he'd put the project on hold because it occurred to him that rejecting the name Susie had given him would wound her.

After the third time Susie went out with Joe, Eric stepped up his surveillance: that is, he googled the man. Maybe an older Italian guy wouldn't have an online presence, but just in case.... And there it was, a well-designed corporate website that immediately offered a chat with an agent.

That night he said to Susie, "Did you know that Joe's, like, a big developer? Townhouses, condos? The coffee shop thing with his niece is just a sideline."

"Sure, he's told me. He's been in real estate for years, done very well at it."

"That's not too, um, capitalist for you? Like, part of the Evil System oppressing the Workers?"

"People need houses to live in, Eric, and somebody has to build them. I didn't construct this house of ours, did you?"

"This place is a hundred years old."

"And a hundred years ago some developer, whoever it was, built the whole block."

"Okay. And that guy was a capitalist. Built 25 little boxes exactly the same to house the wage slaves for the breweries."

"Eric, I know your critique of capitalism is insincere, so stop trying to annoy me. I take people as they are and try to find humanity in everyone."

Eric smirked about this latest example of Susie's inconsistency. Fine, if she wanted to hang with a chubby developer, set her standards that low, no problem. At least she was getting dates, which was more than he was doing.

When a news story broke one Saturday, however, he figured she'd have second thoughts. Joe's current project, Eric learned, was half a block of new condos in the gentrifying neighborhood of Point Breeze, which had been a low-income, depressed, postindustrial area till a recent influx of young professional types. Longtime residents, mostly African Americans, were scared of being pushed out as rents and real estate taxes rose. There'd been some run-ins between old-timers and newcomers, especially because the latter received tax abatements on their pristine condos. In the culture clash of collard greens vs. craft beers, everyone got angry. Even a person with minimal political sensitivity like Eric knew this was a classic gentrification story.

The latest incident, which Eric discovered online at 2 a.m., had taken place at Joe's worksite. A few days ago, a community group had gathered 150 people to protest the development. Not long after, flyers with the message "Smash Gentri Racist Scum" had appeared on dozens of telephone poles. And last night a fire had broken out that destroyed about a quarter of the new construction.

"Oh my god," muttered Susie at the breakfast table, her face bent over her morning paper.

"You reading about the fire?"

"Yeah. They're calling it arson. That's so— ... Wait, how do you know about it?"

"All over social media."

"It's crazy, they could've burnt down the whole block, including the older homes with long-time residents. Thank god no one was hurt. It's one thing to protest— Oh, Joe's quoted here."

Eric poured himself some coffee, sat down, waited while she read.

"And he says ... what?"

"Huh?" Susie's own coffee sat neglected. She had the paper spread on the table, both hands pressing it down, nose hovering a few inches above, so that he saw mostly her sleep-mussed mass of gray hair and the frames of her reading glasses.

"What does Joe say about the arson?"

"I haven't spoken to him today. I'm sure he's really upset."

"In the paper, Mom! You said he's quoted there."

"Oh.... He blamed it on socialist agitators."

"Kind of typical."

"What do you mean, typical?" She raised her face to glare at him.

He flinched backward. "I mean, just, um, that's what I'd expect a developer to say if ... if protesters damaged his property."

"Careless arson is not a protest! And the signs they put up! They called him a racist. This is a man who cares deeply about his Latina niece!"

Eric retreated from arguing with her. If she wanted to brush off the Gentri Racist Scum charges, that was her affair, though of course it violated all her professed principles. A few minutes later, as he fetched himself a bowl of Cheerios, Susie stepped into the living room, and he could hear her making a phone call. He didn't try to eavesdrop, though he knew she was talking to Joe.

The next time she left for an evening, it struck him that she was more dressed up than usual—a skirt rather than jeans, and a pair of dangly, intricate wire earrings. Munching a takeout shrimp burrito, he felt sorry for himself. It seemed unfair that his 66-year-old mother was getting dates while he wasn't, and the potential of a wide-body, bald Italian guy pawing her—if it went that far—felt faintly repulsive. Maintaining neutrality about one's parent's sex life was easier in theory than in practice.

Still, if she fancied a real estate honcho, there was no reason for him to object; he was simply keeping track to make sure she didn't get hurt—although, if it came to that, he didn't have the least notion of how to protect her.

He consoled himself with the burrito (chipotle sauce, pico de gallo, cheese, sour cream, rice, refried beans, lettuce, tomato, onion), and later by going out with some old Hubble Day School friends who were likewise hanging around the city this summer. After three craft beers in a crowded bar, where the friends' witty, ironic banter got squished by the ambient roar, he came home to enjoy raunchy dreams about Melinda.

15

On a Wednesday after school, near the end of the term, Susie sat at the kitchen table slurping coffee and wading through a stack of final essays, which she still required to be printed on paper. Jenna Adelman had submitted a well-written, extremely long but superficial treatise about U.S. support for the 1973 coup in Chile and the murder of Salvador Allende. "Facts nicely arrayed, but a bit short on analysis. Grade: B," Susie scrawled at the end. Thinking she should add a more instructive note, or maybe a plus to the B, she paused awhile before her mind drifted.

She was jittery these days. In the past week there'd been another school gun incident—nearby in fact, but thankfully no one was hurt. An eighth-grade boy in North Philly had been arrested for concealing what might or might not have been an operational handgun in his backpack. Violence was so endemic in some public schools that kids tried to sneak in weapons to protect themselves—usually knives or razor blades—and the root of the problem was obvious. Statistics showed the concentration of poverty worsening in the city, the divisions between rich and poor growing wider and more intractable. Life was near-hopeless for so many, and the capitalist classes continued to do little or nothing about it.

Elsewhere, there'd been more instances of Black people shot by police, and more acts of religious hatred at home and abroad. Worldwide, the news flamed with stories of innocent people displaced and starving. There was also the ongoing disaster of climate change, which the government would never fully address until the Potomac flooded the Capitol, a catastrophe that might prove a blessing.

On top of all this, the state of flux in Susie's personal life disturbed her. These evenings out with Joe—yes, she was enjoying them. Last week, for instance, he'd taken her to the touring version of a Broadway musical, a show beyond her financial reach. Granted, she had little interest in musicals, but the show was fun and some of the tunes still jiggled in her head. He'd also treated her to dinner at expensive restaurants she never would have entered on her own, and the food was superb.

They talked so easily, she might have known Joe for decades. His stories about growing up in an Italian family in Pittsburgh matched what she remembered about her grandparents' house in South Philly. When he described the way GentleGrounds shops donated excess food and a small percentage of profits to the city's leading anti-hunger program, she was impressed. When she expressed shock about the arson at his Point Breeze project, he assured her it was only a temporary setback, and he stressed his commitment to affordable middle-class housing, which he claimed was the opposite of the gentrification he'd been accused of. "In your own neighborhood, up there in Fairmount," he asked, "could you afford to buy your house today?" No, she admitted, and he pointed out that rising prices were good for her if she ever wanted to sell, but bad for young people trying to get a start in life. She and he could even chat about politics, sharing distaste for the complacent corruption that was still all too prevalent in city offices. He showed more interest in her protest activities than she would have expected.

With his friendly attentiveness and persistence in calling her, it felt like she was being courted again, which was kind of unbelievable. Didn't wealthy older men like Joe always date younger women? And hadn't it been in some ways a *relief*, after Julio left, to feel she'd passed beyond male notice? And yet she was incredibly flattered to be treated to dinner and a show and then kissed goodnight—the last time, directly on the lips.

When the little old lady in the mirror gazed back at her, there was astonishment, a smidgen of disapproval and a hint of recklessness. Oh shut up, she told that reflection. And when Errico gave her his glinty-eyed stare from the refrigerator, she glanced away, unsure what to tell him.

All of this played on her nerves, and perhaps that was why the knock at the front door made her jump in her chair. Her knee banged the table leg and her coffee slopped onto Jenna's paper. "Dammit!" she yelled.

Irritably she mopped up the coffee and stretched out the pages to dry, and the rapping came again, longer and louder. When she approached the door at last and saw who it was—the two beefy types, one taller and white, the other shorter and Black—she cursed again, under her breath.

"Now what?" she snapped as she yanked the door open.

"Developments," said Detective Bordick. "Major investigation."

"What is?"

Detective Tate made a small gesture with her hands as if to indicate a spectrum of possibilities. The two cops stood, as before, in the middle of the sidewalk, gazing up at her. Why did they climb the stoop to bang the door and then back away? So annoying—were they afraid she'd burst out with an AK-47 blazing?

"We need to speak with you again," Tate explained. "It shouldn't take long."

"Depends," Bordick asserted, "on who you're protecting."

"He's hiding in plain sight on the refrigerator," Susie countered. "But I don't think you'll get much from him. He died in 1932."

The two detectives frowned and traded puzzled looks.

"May we come in?" Tate asked.

"Or else," Bordick said, "we can talk down at the station. Up to you."

"Oh, for— You have no authority to force me to a police station. But you can come in the house, no problem. We don't need to entertain the neighbors."

As before, Susie pointed them to the living room, where they sat again on the sofa and Tate produced her notepad and pen.

"There's been another incident of violence," Tate began, leaning forward.

"Every day, yes," Susie nodded. "Somebody shot or robbed or raped in this city. I'm sure it keeps you busy."

"We're talking," Bordick burst out, "about setting houses on fire!"

"Houses? Where?"

After a pause, with both detectives watching Susie, Tate said, "A development in the Point Breeze neighborhood."

"Oh," Susie said, "those new condos going up. I saw the story in the paper."

Should she add, she asked herself, that she knew the developer? No, irrelevant.

"We have reason to believe," Tate continued, but Bordick interrupted: "Your pals in black suits! They're up to their necks in this!"

Tate drew a deep breath and blinked, evidently peeved at her partner. Susie too was provoked because he was scuffing his shoe against her coffee table again. How did this ass get to be a detective? Evidence of the Peter principle—promoted to his level of incompetence?

Susie looked back to Tate. "Really? You think it's those people in black? What's your 'reason to believe'?"

"Our evidence"—Tate gave a warning shake of the head to Bordick— "must remain confidential. But it's vital to track down these criminals. Who knows where they'll attack next?"

Susie sighed. "The Point Breeze issue," she explained as if talking to children, "was gentrification, and there've been weeks of protests there, I gather. My group, TeachPeace, was not involved. Gentrification's not part of our agenda. And I've told you, I don't know any of the people in black suits."

"You deny all—" Tate began, but once more her partner interrupted, aggressively crossing his meaty arms: "Obstruction of justice, lady! A serious crime!"

"I'm aware of that," Susie barked back at him. "And if Justice ever shows up in this country, I'll be the first to help her. God knows she'll need assistance."

Tate blinked again, and Bordick let his jaw drop in disgust.

When the detectives got up to leave, Tate handed Susie her card, to which Susie responded, "You gave me one of these already. Maybe I'll put it on my refrigerator for easy reference. If Justice ever drops by, I'll invite you over to meet her."

"Wait," Bordick remembered, "refrigerator? What was that you said about hiding somebody there?"

Tate waved him off as she exited.

* * *

Though the head of Errico praised her handling of the cops, Susie's brain was too agitated to return to grading essays. She reheated a cup of coffee in the microwave and sat brooding at the kitchen table.

"Reason to believe"? What evidence could they have? Surveillance footage again?—but the arson had occurred after dark, when kids in black would be indistinguishable from anyone else. Unless the flames had lit up someone running away? But lots of people wear dark clothes. And it was a poor neighborhood; why would it have cameras—unless Joe had mounted them at his construction site?

This police inquiry could be no more than official paranoia about the Black Bloc. And regardless of the clothing, it likely had nothing to do with Lauren and Sean.

Still, Susie felt abashed at concealing the little she knew—not for obstructing the police (the hell with them) but because Joe or his family had been victimized in both incidents.

A vision of a brick sailing through soft summer air, descending in a gentle arc to splinter flesh and bone. Blood streaming in a brilliant flow ...

No! No! This wasn't her fault, and siccing law enforcement toads like Bordick on naïve kids like Lauren wouldn't improve the situation.

Errico nodded in agreement. With his gift for quoting himself, he reminded her that "the bourgeoisie has no right to complain of the violence of its foes, since its whole history, as a class, is a history of bloodshed."

Yeah, yeah, I know, she replied. But Joe's a nice guy, why should he get the brunt of this?

16

The next night, Susie had the privilege—she considered it that—of meeting Joe's niece Rita and her son Matty. The two lived in one of Joe's South Philly condo developments, a neat, pleasant place that contrasted with Susie's low opinion of condos in general.

Matty bounded around the apartment, playing with a figurine Joe had brought him, a character from the latest sci-fi movie epic. For Susie the boy's appearance was both reassuring (the undiminished energy) and stomach-clenching (the wide bandage that still enveloped his right eye and cheek; the bumpy red scar across his chin).

Joe had also brought a bottle of chianti, which Rita served on her coffee table in broad-bellied glasses. "Susie, thank you so much for your card," she said with a charming hint of a Spanish accent, evidently left over from her childhood in Colombia. "It was such a horrible day, I can hardly think about it, but I know just a few of them attacked my business. People like you meant good."

Rita had a smooth brown complexion, an open face—a pretty young woman. Susie read her concern for her son in the way her dark eyes followed the boy as he dashed through the living room and back toward the kitchen, bouncing the figurine along the walls. Her only child. Susie tried to think how she would have coped if Eric had been terribly injured, disfigured. What could she say?

"It wasn't your business, I mean not yours necessarily, that they picked on. Some of these people, they'll smash anything they associate with capitalism. Then fights broke out in the front with the gun nuts, the crowd got out of hand.... I was there with TeachPeace, we're entirely nonviolent."

"I know, I know. Uncle Joe told me."

"Now they're attacking my condos too," Joe put in. "Bastards."

Susie supported her wine glass with both hands, its bowl was so wide. After a careful sip she said to Rita, "I've been inside the Market Street shop. It's, um, very distinctive. I noticed the way you set up the tables in little groups."

"I'm all about the CX," Rita smiled. "That's what I specialize in."

"CX?"

"Customer experience. What keeps people coming back."

"Oh. Yes, that's smart."

"She's got the big ideas, this girl," Joe beamed, his wine glass engulfed in his large mitt. "The gumption too. Pizzazz."

"With Uncle Joe's help," Rita smiled, turning for an instant to check on Matty.

"Me," he scoffed, "I just handle the business end."

When Susie and Joe got up to leave, Rita gave him a big hug, and Matty jumped into his grand-uncle's arms.

It was such a happy scene, it gave Susie a warm tingle.

17

It was in the spirit of research, Susie told herself, that she noted the cool, smooth, elegant sensation of silk sheets against her legs. The plumpness of the pillow. The lovely soft morning light through deep blue drapes that matched the plush chair in the corner and the comforter crumpled at the foot of the king-size bed.

One could get used to this. Of course Susie didn't think she would. Even if she stayed here many times, high-rise luxury would remain foreign to her inner self. That didn't mean she couldn't enjoy it when an occasion presented itself, and certainly it was useful to study how the one percent lived.

She also noted the slight pressure and muted stimulation from the quiet hand cupping her left breast. She'd never had much in the breast department, and she'd worried that her loss of tone since menopause might be a turnoff. Not for Joe—he'd squeezed and nuzzled as if he couldn't get enough.

Wide awake now, she began to feel sticky where his groin pressed her butt, and her legs cramped because his curled knees prevented her from stretching. Slowly she maneuvered away until, still fast asleep, he flipped onto his back, allowing her to scoot across another yard of mattress to the edge. She snatched up her panties and a dress shirt he'd left on the dresser. The shirt hung practically to her knees, and she had to roll the sleeves way up to liberate her hands.

To avoid disturbing him, she bypassed the bathroom attached to the master bedroom and tiptoed barefoot to the one off the hall. It was outfitted with fixtures so modern and stylish that at first she couldn't decipher how to work the spigot. That conundrum solved, she brushed her teeth with her fingers. When she noticed smeared eyeliner on the face of the little old lady in the mirror, she washed it off, and smiled at herself. For once, last night, she'd allowed herself a touch of makeup, although she'd had to rummage in her closet to find some that she'd used for a theatrical production by Hubble Day teachers and students. Margaret always said she felt naked if she went out without blush and lipstick, but for Susie it was the reverse—artificial aids an embarrassment. Still, in this case ... even Eric had commented favorably on her appearance before she left home.

She'd warned Eric, of course, that she might not return till morning. He'd pursed his lips, started to say something and then refrained. Good sense on his part. What could he have said?

She padded along to the kitchen, a long room with stainless steel appliances and tile floor, a coffered ceiling, all-white cabinets, granite counter tops, a giant built-in refrigerator, a separate breakfast nook as well as a large island with three padded stools, overhung by a filigreed steel chandelier shaped like an upside-down cake. A window in the breakfast area, rising from knee height to the ceiling, offered a vista across miles of city skyline.

After several minutes of eyeing the complicated black machine that might be a coffeemaker, she realized, by a faint aroma, that its insulated pot already held fresh coffee, brewed by timer. She found a mug, filled it and sat down at the teak café-style table to gaze out over the rooftops of ordinary folk. Though the morning was hazy, the view was spectacular, 23 floors up.

She put this quiet time to use by analyzing her feelings, which were mostly cozy despite what she considered the cold, techno nature of the kitchen decor. Last night Joe had cooked her an elaborate dinner of linguini with clams, followed by mustard-crusted bronzino and green beans with lemon and capers, along with two kinds of wine whose names she couldn't remember, and for dessert, lemon semifreddo topped with berries. The pots and pans from his effort still tilted in the left half of the double sink.

It was a wonderful meal, and afterward they'd talked for a long while. Then the transition to bed came easily, the most natural thing in the world. Fears that she couldn't possibly be attractive gave way as Joe proved extraordinarily attentive and solicitous. In the midst of it she wondered why she'd ever abandoned this incredible experience. Since Julio, she'd resigned herself to singleness, but why? Who said she had to?

As for Joe himself, she didn't find him supremely attractive, she didn't want to lick every inch of his body (as she'd tried once with Julio until, tickled beyond endurance, he made her stop), nor did she see him as a soulmate on the deepest level. But he was a very nice person, as she'd told the head of Errico, and she enjoyed being with him. If this were to become a long-term thing, her and Joe—not to get ahead of herself, but *if* … if so, the future seemed less bleak than it had the day she sweltered at Eric's graduation and imagined him 2,800 miles away.

The one glitch last night, if you could call it a glitch, had come when Joe mentioned that he'd driven to Point Breeze that day to check on the rebuild after the fire. They were sitting on the sofa in his giant living room after dinner, with glasses of brandy at hand.

"Is the damage fixed yet?" she asked.

"Naw, it's gonna take weeks. Puts us way behind schedule. And the cops, they haven't said shit. I don't think they're even trying to catch the guy that torched it."

"Oh … I'm sure they're trying." Susie had a momentary impulse to reveal the police visits to her house, but refrained as he put an arm around her.

"I've got cameras up there, and now I'm paying a security detail at night. And if there's any more disturbance, I got a line on who's behind it."

"You mean the community group that was protesting?" Susie adjusted herself under Joe's arm, touching his hand with hers.

"No, I mean one kid in particular, that one at the brunch place."

"Huh?" Susie hesitated. "Oh … Sean? Why would he—"

"I told you I'd seen him before. I remembered he was out there at the site a couple days, yelling louder than the rest, riling up the crazies. Rude language, I won't repeat it. And now I found him on the video."

"Video?"

"At the store. Security camera. The cops looked at the march and the window getting busted, but I wound the video back, checked out earlier dates too. Two days before, there's that kid Sean in front of the shop, hanging by the window. I think he was casing us out so's he could come back in his black gear and mash us up. There's a bit on our corporate website about us being involved with the coffee shops—he must've seen the connection. And then he takes the next step, he torches the place. Also a skinny kid in black, the video's dark but you can just see him slinking off. I told the cops, it's the same guy, but they don't pay attention. I don't think they've done a damn thing."

"Uh … Joe … What makes you think Sean runs around in black?"

"Looks like him on both videos. Skinny like I said, tall, narrow wrists. But when my guys ask around Point Breeze, nobody knows the name. An outside agitator. Too bad all's we have is his first name, no details." Joe turned his head to look at her pointedly.

"Sometimes," Susie murmured, "they use an alias"—true information that was also an evasion.

As he squeezed her upper arm, she suddenly felt sweaty. She wiggled away from him enough to reach her brandy on the coffee table, and after a long sip that drained the glass, she said, "Joe, I scarcely know that boy, or what he's capable of—and I never saw him," she lied, "wearing black…. Anyway, there's a big step from breaking windows to arson."

"I don't know about that," he disputed, but then he got up to fetch them both more brandy, and when he returned to the sofa, they moved to other topics, and soon the snuggling started in earnest.

Now, as she gazed out the kitchen window at the cloud-smeared horizon, a patch of naked skin appeared in the corner of her eye, and she spun around to find Joe in nothing but plaid boxer shorts, his massive chest matted with black and gray hair, his legs also hirsute but skinny in comparison, his belly a round pale bloom.

She stood up to greet him, restraining her impulse to laugh. She loved the fact that he'd appear in such unpretentious form.

He spoke first. "You look great this morning."

This amused her too, it was so absurd; and yet she almost felt it might be true. "Yeah," she said, extending one bare leg, "it always works in the movies. There's nothing more fetching than a hot young actress in underpants and a man's shirt."

"Gimme a hug, my hot young actress. Mmmmm."

She did. Plus, since she had finger-brushed her teeth and needn't fear morning-mouth, a kiss.

"I was going to make us coffee," she said, "but your machine beat me to it. My place isn't so automated."

"You don't have a coffee pot with a timer? That's way-old technology. Wait'll you see this." He strode toward the stove. "Miranda," he gruffly ordered, "make us two omelets with goat cheese and sundried tomato."

"Miranda?"

"The next generation of home assistants." He removed two plates from a cabinet and held them out flat, hands extended over the gleaming stovetop. Susie stared in shocked anticipation.

After a minute, he grinned over his shoulder. "Damn, I guess she's not woke up yet. We'll have to make the omelets ourselves. You up for chopping onion?"

Susie exhaled but refused to admit she'd been taken in. "I'm pondering," she said, "why home assistants have female names."

"'Cause who'd want an omelet made by Melvin? Eggs're in the fridge. There oughta be fresh basil in the crisper. You game?"

They chopped and whipped together, and Joe displayed his expertise at flipping omelets at exactly the right moment.

"Where'd you learn to cook?"

"My nonna. I told you about her."

While they ate, the sun dissolved the clouds, and the cityscape came up bright through the window: apartment towers, church spires, lines of row houses down below, a streak of river twisting round a curve. The view added to Susie's joy as she stuffed herself with onion-basil-feta-tomato omelet, toast with marmalade, coffee and orange juice.

Joe added the dirty dishes to his pile in the sink. "I'll take care of these later." He laid a soft paw on her shoulder. "Now, any chance I can get you back to bed?"

"Oh, god. I'm, uh, flattered, but I don't think I'd, mmm, survive. Give me some time to recuperate.… Anyway, I should get home, dear, I'm wading through my students' final essays. I hate giving grades, but the school insists."

Joe sighed, stretching his furry arms. Watching his belly shimmy, she had a surge of affection, more motherly than erotic. Truly a nice man, but at this instant she wanted to be in her own modest home, away from steel appliances and gleaming white cabinets. And she longed for her own shower.

"Yeah," he said, "I gotta work too. Get down to Point Breeze, check where they left off yesterday."

While she returned to the bedroom to dress, he began a kitchen clean-up. When she emerged, he stopped banging pots and pans to come over and wrap his arms around her. She playfully ran her fingernails down his bare back.

"I do hope everything's all right at your construction site."

"Should be. Anyway, I'm not waiting any longer on the cops, I'm gonna take care of it myself. Meanwhile, gimme another hug?"

She did, and he tousled her freshly combed hair.

"Okay, lemme throw some clothes on and I'll drive you home."

"No no, I like the bus. Nothing against your Lexus, but I *like* the bus, I really do. Public transit is the wave of the future."

He pretended to make a face, then pleaded, "Can I call you soon?"

"Nobody's stopping you," she grinned, and gave his soft white belly a farewell pat.

18

Later that Saturday morning, as Susie resumed grading essays at her kitchen table, there was a lingering sweetness from the night with Joe, a kind of mild, satisfied flow of energy through her body. She was *happy*, a feeling she didn't remember having in the past few months. At the same time, disturbing eddies swirled around the edges.

Around noon she heard Eric stirring, and when he came downstairs for a meal that might be called breakfast, if two bananas and a quart of orange juice qualified as such, she expected him to say something about her night away from home—an acknowledgment, at least, that he'd noticed. But he said little at all, and absolutely nothing about that.

She wondered if his silence amounted to criticism. And when he clumped back to his room with the orange juice carton (she'd given up asking him to use a glass), she couldn't focus again on her task. Getting up, she began to fix herself some lunch—just cheese and crackers, since she still felt full from Joe's elaborate breakfast.

At this point, some of her small disturbances rose into larger waves.

She heard Joe's voice again: "I'm gonna take care of it myself," he'd said about the two attacks on his properties. He'd made it clear he thought the cops were useless, and he meant to take matters into his own broad hands. What did that mean?

Susie had no affection for Sean or desire to protect him. Still, he might be guilty of nothing more than stupidity, and even if he *was* guilty of one or both crimes, she wouldn't, on principle, want a professed anarchist persecuted for actions against the system, however misguided. Yet also, on principle, she didn't condone violence that injured innocent people or threatened their homes.

On still another principle, she felt it'd be wrong for Joe to go off half-cocked, blaming Sean without any direct evidence that he did anything at all except run around in a black costume (which Joe didn't know for sure) and shout antifascist rhetoric.

What it came down to was: should she warn Lauren?

Was there anything concrete to warn Lauren about?

What could Joe do?

Joe was a law-abiding citizen, he wouldn't get out of hand.

Besides, what obligation did she have to Lauren beyond thanking her for a minor good deed, which was only what anyone should have done under the circumstances?

As she munched her cheese and crackers, she tried discussing the matter with the head of Errico, but he proved surprisingly inert this morning. His slight smirk seemed to gaze into the distance beyond her.

After lunch, Susie called Margaret and told her, in vague terms, about the night with Joe, and her friend, while pretending not to be amazed, was glad and supportive. "Wow!" Margaret said, "I didn't know it was that serious." The two friends chatted for half an hour, and Susie failed to mention her moral quandary.

Though she generally detested music in the background while she worked, Susie put on her *Songs of the Spanish Civil War* for comfort as she returned to her exam forms.

> *Give us victory, or give us death.*
> *The cause we're fighting for is noble:*
> *To free all men from slavery's chains.*

Rousing words, but what did they mean in the present circumstances?

She didn't call or text Lauren. And for the next week she didn't hear from Joe. The sudden absence of his attention left her both agitated and subdued. Should she phone him? No, he might suggest another sleepover, and she wasn't sure she was ready for that—although it *would* be nice, wouldn't it? Especially if he cooked her dinner again.

19

At first Eric thought Rita Gutierrez's return to the store would improve the environment. She was friendlier than her Uncle Joe and much more attentive to the work that people were doing. Besides, with her long dark hair and big warm eyes, she was a treat to look at. She could rock an apron!

By the end of the first week, though, he had his doubts. Yes, she was always cheerful, talkative, relentlessly positive, darting around to tease the employees and engage with customers. But she also micromanaged the details, reminding the staff every ten minutes to check the milk canisters, clear tables immediately, pick up dropped napkins, wipe spills from the counter, empty the trash cans at least once an hour even if they weren't halfway full.... Sheesh.

It was all about the CX, she said in her rapid-fire speech, and for several days Eric understood that term as a lightly Latin-inflected pronunciation of "sex," which to him suggested an interesting but opaque concept. In what way did clean tables connote (or promote) sex? A full canister of cream meant ... what, exactly?

Eventually, when snotty Melissa clued him in, he had to hide his disdain. "Customer Experience"? In his view, 90 percent of the customers wanted caffeine, not experience—for the harried business types, the less "experience" the better.

And then there was the incident of the malfunctioning cash register. The machine was super high-tech and super fragile. If you looked at it from the wrong angle, it'd freeze up. That one day, it went down for two hours, and while they waited for the repair geek, Rita quickly devised a substitute cash-only system. Here, she showed the staff, on this pad of paper you write the amount of each item in the order; then use this handheld calculator to add them up; write the total here; read the state and city tax off this chart and add that to the total; when the customer gives you cash, subtract like this ... and so on. Some of the employees struggled to follow any system not based on electronics and plastic cards, and their arithmetic made it doubtful they'd graduated from third grade.

Eric of course had no trouble with the numbers, nor did he need to write down simple calculations, and he considered it cruelly ironic that his ability got him in trouble. During a sudden flurry of orders, Rita happened to be standing nearby when a customer asked for an egg sandwich with cheddar on a pumpernickel bagel, a side of tempeh bacon and a 16-ounce soy latte with mocha syrup. The man casually handed a $20 bill to Eric, who just as casually and automatically handed back four ones, three quarters and three pennies.

The man looked puzzled. Rita erupted at what she thought was sloppy approximation on Eric's part. After a long exchange, during which the customer professed to be satisfied—"No big deal, it seems about right"—and Rita took precious minutes, holding up the line, to write down each basic component and each modification—$1.00 extra for cheddar, $.50 for syrup—Eric was vindicated, to the penny. The man dropped a dollar in the tip jar. Yet Rita marched away in a huff, and by then some of the waiting customers had walked out.

It reminded Eric of the time in fifth grade when a teacher had given him a C on a test, though every answer was perfect, because he failed to "show his work." There hadn't been any work!

Though he eventually smoothed things over with Rita, he was relieved on Friday morning to see Uncle Joe instead. Rita had to take Matty to the hospital for a follow-up, the staff was told, and the store settled back into what Eric considered its "old" routine: cleaning when there was actual dirt, filling milk canisters when they were actually empty, etc. Joe mostly stayed in the back talking on the phone.

But having been conditioned by Rita's hyper personality, and feeling bored during a slow period, Eric found himself changing the trash bag next to the condiment station despite the 8 inches of space left in it. He hauled the old bag, plus two from the kitchen, through a long blank hallway to the dumpster in the back alley. Leaning on the cool metal of the dumpster, he debated whether it'd be proper to loaf here for five minutes—the smokers got to take breaks for smoking, didn't they? wasn't that discrimination against nonsmokers? On the other hand, the odor here wasn't particularly pleasant. Maybe this was a reason for smoking, so you could stand by garbage without smelling it.

As he contemplated whether this rationale—blocking out the noxious world—might be the key to other weird personal tastes like his ex-semi-girlfriend's attraction to Percy Bysshe Shelley, he noticed a tiny red car with a white roof angling around the miscellaneous parked delivery trucks. When it stopped about thirty yards away, two beefy men in dark T-shirts got out. The sight was kind of amusing, such big guys emerging from a minuscule vehicle, like a clown car in a circus. Eric had never been to a circus—his mother detested their "exploitation" of both animals and people—but he'd seen videos online.

While his mind shifted to the philosophical status of circus acts—did elephants really mind carrying half-naked women around a ring? why would that be objectionable?—a third man approached the others and handed one of them an envelope, which was quickly stuffed into a coat pocket. Oh, that third dude was Joe—when had he come out? In a few seconds the burly men wedged themselves back into the little coupe, which then backed up, turned and sped away. Idly, Eric noticed the numbers on the license plate, 1597, and then he scooted back into the building before Joe could catch him loitering.

As he loped back through the long hallway, he grinned, recognizing certain properties of the number 1597. It was a prime, a Fibonacci number and an emirp too. Wait, wasn't it the largest known Fibonacci emirp?

For the rest of his shift, he entertained himself by pondering the fascinating features of 1597, becoming so lost in the mathematical beauty that he worked an extra 12½ minutes by mistake. Along the way, it occurred to him that Nasrin Sassani would have to be impressed by knowledge of this sort—wouldn't she?

III

With office towers and the Convention Center blocking his view, William Penn could not have witnessed the odd little scene a few blocks from his sturdy bronze feet. Diagrammed, it would have resembled a dance sequence on the brightly lit summer stage, two dancers emerging from a small box to circle another two. The first two closed on one, and three became a single rotating mass while the fourth spun off to the side. When the cluster flew apart, the first two returned to their box and sped off stage right, while the third and fourth remained on stage, splayed horizontally. A peculiar ballet that would have struck Penn as bizarre and disorderly.

20

After her last, wrapping-up day of the school year on Friday, Susie looked forward to a big glass of iced coffee and a rest on her sofa. The weather had turned scorching again, and the short trek from the bus stop had left her exhausted. But just as her key touched the front-door lock, she was attacked from behind.

The assault was verbal, but with the force of physical blows. She staggered and nearly fell down her stoop.

The assailant had materialized out of thin air, and at first Susie couldn't make sense of the screaming.

When she steadied herself with a shaky hand on the railing, she looked down at the sidewalk and saw who it was, and some of the words became intelligible.

"You sicced them on us! You told that bastard where to find us!"

"What're you yelling about? Calm down!!! What's the matter with you?"

The young woman glared up at Susie, her teeth mauling her upper lip as if she'd like to do that to Susie's face. "Pretending you're part of the movement! When you're in league with the fascist corporate pigs!!"

"Jesus fucking Christ, Lauren," Susie cursed, breaking her own rule about proper reverence for the word *fuck*. "Shut your mouth a minute!"

Though Lauren showed no inclination to obey, she paused her invective, hands defiantly on her hips, chin thrust up.

Susie gasped a sigh. "You're not going to hit me, are you?" Susie glanced up and down the block, seeing no neighbors around to protect her. But why should she be afraid—this was just a silly young girl. "Look, how about … if you … get control of yourself. Come in the house and we can talk about whatever's—"

The response was somewhere between an expectoration and a growl.

"How did you know my address anyway?"

Now the words spat like a stream of rocks. "You're fucking *easy* to find, but *we* try to stay *underground*. Till people give us away! They busted both of his knees! Right in front of our apartment!"

"Ohmigod. You mean … ?" Susie's gut wrenched. "Let's go in. Quick, c'mon, off the street."

Susie hustled the girl inside and pointed her to the living-room sofa. Lauren paced around the room, sat down, stood up, sat again and crossed her legs and arms, then lowered her head and began sobbing. Since she was dressed in a sleeveless blue top, the tears ran down her arms, a few dropping onto her shorts and bare knees.

"I don't know why I'm here," she moaned, her vocal cords crackling. "You're a fucking stool pigeon."

"Tell me what happened," Susie urged, sitting on the sofa at a safe distance.

"Don't you know? Do you care?"

"I *don't* know. I do *care*, I think, but until you tell me what's ..."

"There was another protest at your pal's *fucking* new condos this morning. So we get back, and these two *goons* jump us. Thugs in black T-shirts. One had a baseball bat! They grabbed Sean and smashed both his knees, one then the other. It was like—like explosions! firecrackers! Oh fucking shit it's so so fucking *awful.*"

Susie agreed, and now she could see the right side of Lauren's forehead, red and swollen.

"And you were hurt too? It looks like—"

"Me, shit, it's nothing, my head hurts, one guy threw me down. *Threw* me! But Sean—a shop owner called 911, an ambulance came. I went over to the hospital and they said he's ... it's *bad*, like, both knees totally wrecked, bones and ligaments and stuff, it's gonna be weeks before he can even— He was so out of it he couldn't talk to me."

"Shh, shh," said Susie, her stomach trembling. She reached out to touch Lauren's shoulder.

The young woman violently shook the hand away. "And you fucking told them where to find us!"

"I did not!" Susie rallied to defend herself. "Obviously they tailed you from the demonstration."

"Fucking *not* obvious! We're careful, we never take a direct route."

"Did the cops come too? What did you tell them?"

"Zilch. I ducked 'em."

"What's the noise about?" said another voice.

It was Eric, emerged from his afternoon nap.

Susie tried to wave Eric away, then realized it was futile. "This is my son," she explained. "Eric, this is Lauren. Her boyfriend was just beaten up, badly hurt. She thinks it's because he—"

Susie stopped, not wanting to involve Eric in connections that she hoped were entirely speculative.

After one dismissive glance at the intruder, Lauren accused Susie, "I bet you'd recognize their car. Maybe it's your boyfriend's own car. *One* of his cars, he must have twenty."

"What are you talking about?"

"The car the fucking goons drove! Here, I got a picture when they fucked off!"

Lauren extracted a phone from the tight front pocket of her shorts. After a couple of thumb taps, she held it out to Susie. "A bright red Mini with a white roof. Brand new, looked like. A toy car for a honcho fucking capitalist Nazi."

Susie stared at the phone, not quite grasping the image at first. Taken from a low angle—evidently from where Lauren had been thrown on the sidewalk—it showed just a hunk of red rear fender and trunk. Then she noticed: "Oh, you got part of the license plate! Seven at the end. The number before that—is it an eight? If you're sure it's a Mini, the police might be able to—"

"The cops? They're in bed with the thug capitalists."

"Wait, can I see that?" Eric, who'd been standing with hands in his jean pockets, looking simultaneously sleepy and hungry if that were possible, lunged forward and stretched a long arm toward the phone.

"Why the fuck are you— That's *my* phone," Lauren objected, but Susie shut her down with an emphatic gesture.

When Eric glanced at the picture, he said, "Oh, it's 1597."

"What?" said Susie.

"The number on the license plate. It's 1597."

"You can't *see* the whole number. It's not visible."

"But I saw it around noon."

As the two women stared at him, Eric's expression changed from curious to mildly alarmed. "Um," he said, "what exactly is this about? You said *goons*?"

Explanations followed, including how and when Eric had seen this car, or a nearly identical one, and who had engaged with the men inside it.

When his mother challenged his memory of random digits, he went into detail about the number's meaningfulness, going so far as to fetch a pencil and paper to start listing the sequence of Fibonacci primes. He also showed them that 1597, written backwards, formed another prime, making it an emirp (*prime* spelled backwards, he explained with a touch of condescension).

"Okay, okay," Susie cut him off. "What's the point of this?"

"A lotta wacko crap," Lauren grumbled, her voice descending into full scratchiness.

"The *point*," Eric said rather haughtily, "is that primes form fascinating patterns. Nobody quite understands them, but there are tons and tons of conjectures. So if I see an interesting one on a license plate—"

"Never mind, Eric," Susie sighed, trying to calm herself enough to parse things out. "Look … if we accept that you remember the numbers on the plate, and it's really the same car"—Susie resisted the links that were becoming all too clear—"is there any chance you remember the letters too? The colors show it's a Pennsylvania plate, so there'd be three letters before the numbers."

"Letters?" Squatting by his list of primes on the coffee table, Eric looked puzzled, as if letters were a foreign language. He squinched his eyes, apparently trying to visualize the license plate, but had to give up. "No," he said, "no letters. They weren't interesting."

"Anyway," Susie reasoned, "with all four numbers, the police can—"

"Nuh-uh!" Lauren burst out. "No fucking cops! Don't you dare tell them anything!"

21

Lauren didn't leave. Which was sort of okay with Eric because she was attractive in a way, not pretty but sexy with her long dark hair, skinny frame and perky small breasts. With tear tracks on her face and a bruise on her brow, she looked kind of fetching, to which her foul mouth added an interesting fillip. And though she'd referred to mathematics as wacko crap, he wouldn't necessarily pass up a chance to educate her. He imagined that creaky, crackly voice murmuring softly as he explained the magical behavior of the number 17, for instance.

During dinner (turkey burgers with a green salad and applesauce), he learned that Lauren was the one who'd treated Susie's wound after the march. That bolstered his willingness to give the girl a chance, but it didn't explain the peculiar hostile/friendly bond she seemed to have with his mother. Of course, Susie's personal relationships had always been impossible to fathom—like her fancy for Joe, of all people.

When he wasn't checking out Lauren's body, he studied his mom. She seemed to be moving with care, taking her time—holding the plate of burgers over the stove for 30 seconds before turning to set it on the kitchen table. She didn't talk much. Well, if her new love interest was linked with goons who went around bashing people's knees for—as far as Eric understood—merely demonstrating against condos, no wonder she was upset.... But he sensed there was a lot they weren't telling him. He fretted that his naive little bourgeois anarchist mother had been pulled into something dangerous because she couldn't pass up any worthy cause: gun control, poverty, police brutality, immigration, voting rights, climate change ... it was hard sometimes to know what *wasn't* a cause.

At least this girl Lauren didn't seem an immediate threat. After grumbling that she was mostly vegan, she gobbled two burgers with thick toppings of mustard. Her forehead was gradually turning purple. She said something about going back to the hospital to see Sean, who Eric supposed was the busted-knee boyfriend, but after the meal she went instead to the sofa and turned on the TV. Hoping for further explanation, Eric helped Susie clear the dishes and tidy the kitchen, but all he got from his mother were ironic glances deriding his sudden attention to domestic chores.

He retreated to his room, where he thought of another step he could take: a deeper web search on Joe Sambucco. The first time, he'd let himself be pulled in by the early hits, especially the development corporation's site. Now he explored further: the name led to an Italian bistro, a rock band, a cannoli recipe, an obituary, a genealogical site—two, three pages of irrelevant crud.

Finally, a single unpromising line linked to an archived, blurry, partial image from a local newspaper in western Pennsylvania 24 years ago. Eric stared at it for five minutes. Then he carried his laptop downstairs.

Susie sat stiffly beside Lauren on the couch, much as he'd found them this afternoon. But they weren't talking. Lauren's eyes were glommed onto a reality show blaring on TV while Susie had her head down, hands folded in her lap. Eric managed to attract his mother's notice and beckoned her over by the front door.

"Look at this."

"I don't understand, Eric. What is it?"

"Read it. Here, I'll make it bigger."

His mother squinted to read the screen without her glasses:

> On Thursday morning federal agents raided the real estate office of Joseph P. Sambucco, 44, of Springdale, in connection with the ongoing probe of the Melchionni crime family.
>
> Officers were seen removing a dozen or more boxes of records and two computers. According to an official source, a warrant was issued to gather evidence of alleged money laundering for illegal gambling operations in the Valley.
>
> Following the early-morning raid, employees locked the door of the realty company and declined to comment when reached by

At that point the image was cut off.

Eric said, gently, "Doesn't have to be the same Joe. This story's from the western part of the state.… Did he ever live out there?"

"Joe? He said he grew up near Pittsburgh. I don't know when he came to Philly, I think a long time ago."

"This is from over 24 years ago, so the person that's 44 in this article would be 68 now, or 69, depending on the date of his birthday."

"Yeah."

"So … how old is Joe?"

Susie drew a deep breath through her nose. "I don't know exactly."

"What's his middle initial?"

"I don't think he uses one."

Eric refrained from saying, "There's a lot you don't know about this dude you're sleeping with." He kept his mouth closed and waited, though it hurt his back to bend over enough for his mother to see the screen.

She continued to study it, and eventually she murmured, "What you're suggesting is … if he wanted to, to rough somebody up, he knew the right people to call. Mob guys."

"I didn't say that."

"Right, you didn't say, but you came down to show me this…. How did you find it?"

"It's on the internet, Mom. Anyone can find it."

They left the matter there, and Susie returned to the sofa, where she again sat zombie-like next to Lauren.

Hours later, Eric heard from his mother that Lauren was "scared to go home tonight. She's a nervous wreck."

"Scared of the goons coming back? But if we give the cops the license plate—"

"No. Absolutely not. She refused."

Eric shrugged. Again there seemed to be much that people weren't telling him.

Despite his skepticism, he offered to give up his bed for the girl. "I'll sleep on the sofa," he declared in Lauren's presence. "It's kind of short for me, but I'll make do," he added, to make sure his gallantry was appreciated.

"First," said Susie, "you'll have to clear a path in your room, through the comic books on the floor."

"They're not comic books, they're graphic fantasy novels. And there *is* a path."

"Just pick them up, would you?"

22

By noon the next day, Saturday, Lauren had disappeared from the house, and Eric too had made himself scarce, though he wasn't scheduled to work. Susie sat alone in her kitchen with the heroic head of Malatesta, whose advice that "Impossibility never prevented anything from happening" only made the situation seem more impossible.

Had Joe not called for a week because he knew she'd disapprove of his revenge on Sean? Did he realize she'd find out? Was it her fault because she hadn't acted to stop him? Should she be concerned about Lauren? What was she supposed to do about any of this?

The brick, launched by her own arm, met little resistance from the skin and supple young bones.

Her dizziness suddenly returned, and as she pressed both hands against her skull to steady herself, a series of persistent notes rang in her head. The lightheadedness was turning to noise? Was this a punishment for—?

Only when the sound ceased did she realize it was her phone on the counter. She stood up to retrieve it, steadying herself against the wall, the stove. When she recognized Lauren's number on the screen, she sat down again and returned the call, her fingers trembling.

"Shit, shit, shit," the girl answered.

"Good afternoon to you, too, Lauren." Susie forced her voice toward calm while, with her free hand, she jabbed three fingers against her skull, applying pressure.

"That's what my life is now."

"Welcome to the club."

"Because you know what he wants me to do?"

Susie took a sharp breath.

"Go back there at night and break stuff. 'Cause we shouldn't let the creep get away with this."

"Wait, wait. This is Sean telling you to go … to go back to the condos and damage them?"

"Don't say names on the phone. They could be tapping—"

"Listen, I bet the security at—the security *there*, is really intense now. Don't you go near that place."

"You think I'm fucking *crazy*? After what they did to him?"

"So you didn't tell him you'd—"

"I am *not* fucking *crazy*!!!! But he's pressuring me to— He yanked my arm and I fell against one of his knees. He screamed, the nurses came running in …"

"Ugh."

"And when they left—they were accusing me, telling me not to lean on the bed, don't put any pressure on the—what the fuck, do they think I'm a moron?"

"Where are you now?"

A long pause. "At the apartment," Lauren finally squeezed out. "But I can't stay here."

"Why not? If he's laid up in the hospital awhile …"

"It's *his* place, he pays the rent from his job at the hardware store. It's kind of our deal, he helps me with school tuition if I go with him to— He's only got the one other member."

"Maxie?"

"How do you know that name!"

"He said it once. Listen, Lauren, don't let him bully you. It's your apartment too, no matter who pays the rent."

"The goons could come back! Besides, the whole place *reeks* of him. I can smell the fucking peanut butter he eats out of the jar—Skippy, which is like the most processed, sugary, chemical stuff ever!"

The girl's agitation annoyed Susie as much as it worried her. "Where are your parents?" Susie pressed. "Brothers, sisters? Can't you stay with—"

"I don't talk to them!!"

"How about friends?"

Angry muttering.

The old saw came to mind: You made your bed, now lie in it. Then another image of the flying brick flashed by. Susie had more in common with this mindless young woman than she wanted to admit.

"Lauren … ," Susie hesitated. "Listen, you can come back here if you need to."

"My elbow hurts where he wrenched it so hard, I think I'll have a bruise like the one on my head!"

"Lauren, listen to me. Come back to my house. Pack a bag, will you, and get over here. We'll sort this out together."

* * *

Before Lauren arrived, Susie realized she couldn't handle matters alone. Not today, with so much whirling in her head, and her head whirling on her body. She phoned Margaret.

"Honey," she said, "are you busy tonight? Is there any chance you can come over for dinner?"

"Oh. This is sudden. You're not going out with Joe tonight?"

"No."

"What's the occasion then?"

"No occasion.... No, that's not exactly.... Complicated reasons. Somebody I need you to meet. To help me figure things out."

"It does sound complicated. Does this offer come with your baked ziti?"

"It could."

"I'll bring dessert. Six o'clock?"

23

Eric was always pleased to see his Aunt M, as he called her, and this time she came bearing a graduation gift, a boxed hardcover set of a classic fantasy trilogy from the early 2000s, newly illustrated. It was the sort of treasure he would not, for an instant, leave on the floor of his bedroom.

"Oh man, I've seen this but couldn't afford it. This artist—she's, like, collected in museums! Thank you, Aunt M!" Eric bent down from his perch on the arm of the sofa to hug her.

"I've been waiting for a chance to give it to you. You know I would've come to the ceremony if I wasn't out of town for my grandbaby's birthday."

"You didn't miss anything. Long boring speeches."

"That is so cool," murmured Lauren from the far end of the sofa, peering across at the books.

"You like fantasy novels too?" Margaret asked.

"Who doesn't?"

"Well, Eric is well supplied."

"Yeah, I've seen. On the floor, on the shelves, in the closet, under the bed."

"You two have a lot in common in that department."

Eric, blushing, tried to signal Margaret by blinking and wiggling his chin, but she proved oblivious. Luckily his mother called from the kitchen, "Dinner in five! Eric, finish setting the table, please!"

As Lauren headed toward the bathroom, Eric lingered to whisper fiercely to Margaret, "She's *not* my girlfriend. That's not why she's here."

"Oh? Was I implying that? Too bad, she's kind of—"

"She's the one that patched Mom's ear after the march last month."

"Oh."

"But it looks like Joe hired Mafia thugs to bust up her boyfriend."

"*What?*"

In a hurry Eric tried to fill in the details, such as he understood them, before his mother nagged him again about the table. Margaret's face moved from alarm to deep bewilderment.

* * *

Since the dining table was only the kitchen table repurposed, with actual place settings rather than strewn cutlery, it was a cozy arrangement for four. The air conditioner valiantly kept the oven heat at bay while the wild-haired Malatesta cast a benevolent gaze from the refrigerator.

Unlike Susie, whose probes often felt pointed, Margaret had a gentle way of drawing people out. With her large comfortable presence and good-hearted manner, she could explore the most personal topics with a minimum of resistance. Over the baked ziti, crunchy kale salad and warm garlic bread, she worked this technique on Lauren.

"I'm so glad you were there to help Susie at the Disarm Hate rally. We were supposed to meet up, but we messed up our text messages—or I did, I guess."

"No problem," Lauren said, the tip of a kale leaf poking onto her lower lip. "I'm in nursing school, I know how to treat a cut."

"Still, in all the chaos, you had the presence of mind, that's something.... How long before you graduate?"

Lauren had to manage a huge mouthful of ziti from her loaded plate before she could answer. "Another year," she swallowed. "Or so. Depending on tuition."

"Oh. You mean ... raising money for tuition? It's expensive, I know. Are you at Temple?"

"Ummm, have been, yeah."

"It's a long-term crisis," said Susie, "the price of education in this country. I've been thinking TeachPeace should address the problem."

"After," Eric broke in, and then mumbled, "all the other ones." He suppressed a cynical comment about the long list of his mother's causes, realizing this would sound wrong from someone who'd ridden scholarships through school. Nodding his head, he took a chomp of garlic bread.

"Do you live up near Temple, dear?" Margaret pursued.

"Uh ... no ... I've been at my, my boyfriend's apartment, but he's kind of—"

"Laid up at the moment," Susie bailed her out. "In the hospital."

"That's a shame. At least with your training you can help—"

"If he wants me around," Lauren muttered savagely, stabbing three pieces of ziti.

Eric saw Margaret's eyes move from Lauren to Susie and back again as if she didn't know which presented the larger puzzle.

In this jagged way, the conversation continued through the German chocolate cake that Margaret had brought—Lauren attacked that, too, acting like she hadn't eaten well for a month—and by the end of dessert, Margaret had drawn out some of the girl's background.

"Run the latest White People's Fashionable Disease Campaign," the girl said, to the question of what her parents did. "Dr. and Mrs. Steven W. Humphrey of Malvern. Surely you've seen them in the Society columns?"

Margaret offered a quizzical smile.

"The third Mrs. Dr. Humphrey," the girl added, with deeper sarcasm. "Elegant in pink. Twenty-three years his junior."

"Mmm," Margaret nodded. "If I ever have a fashionable disease, I'll be grateful. But I don't think my arthritic knee qualifies."

"No," the girl's voice scratched into its lowest register, "ordinary people never qualify in Little Pink Bitch's world." She then looked abashed, as if she'd been rude, but Margaret and Susie exchanged looks of concern, and Eric merely felt the girl was irrational. In his view there was no point in hating your parents if they could have financed your schooling.

After dinner, while Eric again helped his mother with the dishes, Margaret took Lauren to the living room to continue their chat. Still later, when Lauren went upstairs to his room—now apparently her room for an unspecified period—Eric, displaced, sat alone in the kitchen playing with his phone while Susie and Margaret huddled on the sofa.

"What a lost soul," he heard Margaret say at one point. "What are you going to do about her? And about Joe?"

24

Despite the comfort of an evening with Margaret, Susie didn't sleep well. She was back in the commune, stirring and stirring the stinky stock pot. When she looked inside it was empty, but there was no escape from her duty to stir and stir and stir. Old Papa Dump sat in the corner leering at her, and when he spoke, he talked about the new condos he was building. Greg lay splayed on the kitchen floor—was he dead or merely acting out one of his theater pieces? Glass shattered, and then the house was burning. Marty Leffler ran by with his clarinet, playing a Pied Piper tune, and a horde of bandaged children followed him, limping on broken knees.

In the morning she knew—Margaret had helped her understand—that she had decisions to make, but after the night of nightmare-ridden, sticky-hot tossing and turning, she was in no mood to face them.

Fumbling groggily in the shower, she dropped the soap, and after she bent to fetch it and straightened again, a wave of vertigo tipped her hard against the tiles. Her feet skidded; she began to fall.

She saw it at once: bleeding from a broken head, naked on the shower floor—how humiliating!

They'd come and carry her away, just as they'd carried the cop long ago. He wasn't naked, of course. He'd stood in full uniform, with a baton in hand. But the brick had curved over the poised baton, its edge catching him right in the eye. From a distance she saw the blood gush, the big body crumple....

In fact she didn't fall. She caught herself with hands splayed against the shower wall, inched out with her head down, sank onto the toilet seat, dripping everywhere—water, not blood.

In a few minutes the dizziness passed, but its sudden return had left her flustered. How could she face what she had to face if this weakness ...

She dressed carefully, clean jeans, clean blouse; it seemed important to present herself well today. Even so, she crept by the closed door of Eric's room, not wanting to wake the girl. Likewise, when she found Eric snoring on the sofa, she tiptoed past him to the kitchen with only a quick glance at his awkward posture. In boxer shorts and T-shirt, he had one long leg hooked over the sofa back, the other poking out beyond the armrest, his head propped sideways—impossibly uncomfortable for anyone but her son.

He was the least of her worries. To suppress her shuddering thoughts, she fixated on the ritual of coffeemaking. Put the kettle on. Measure the beans. Grind them. (Check that the noise didn't wake Eric—fat chance.) Pluck a paper filter from the box, unfold it in the cone. Dampen it with warm water. Place the cone on the glass pot, tip in the ground beans, wait patiently for the water to boil. It was a slow, detailed process—no such thing as an automated timer like Joe's. No view of the city out the window, only the scrawny bushes in pots around her tiny brick yard, wilted from days of heat. No sleek white cabinets, just old nicked wooden ones.

When the water boiled, she concentrated on pouring it into the cone, not too fast, not too slow, a steady stream. She had brewed coffee this way for—how long was it? Since her first semester of college.

She had to sort things out. *Too, too much violence.* The image of Sean's crushed knees— But there were distinctions to be made. Things had to be *separated.*

She placed her full cup, strong and black, on the kitchen table, and then, wobbly again, sank into a chair.

From the side of the refrigerator, the face of Malatesta gazed impassively. He had been besieged by illness throughout his life, and yet he had carried on with his good work. Always an inspiration, a model for her.

Yet after one sip of coffee, she buried her head in her hands.

* * *

Over the course of an hour, primed with three cups of coffee, punctuated by occasional sleep-snorts from the living room, the thoughts arranged themselves, not entirely clear but in a semblance of order.

The crowbar smashing a store window, with a little boy seriously wounded, perhaps disfigured: this was meant as an attack on property—ill-timed and stupid, but the injury had been accidental.

Arson at the condos, also aimed at property. Even more senseless because, if the fire got out of hand, neighbors could've been killed. Thankfully the fire was contained in time, nobody hurt.

And then a kneecapping—was that what they called it? Bloody, vicious personal attack. Horrid! Margaret too had been appalled to hear of it.

And the issues of responsibility:

Whether Sean broke the window—likely.

Whether Sean set the fire—at this point, probable. Margaret's quizzing of Lauren had revealed that she and Sean had lived in Point Breeze until they were pushed out by rising rents. Lauren had uttered some bitter words about rich absentee landlords. Since Sean seemed the type to hold big grudges, he would take that attitude to an extreme.

Validity of the protests against the condos—complicated. Gentrification was often evil, no doubt about it, but arson went way beyond justification.

Whether Joe ordered the attack on Sean—how likely? If true, inexcusable!

All of this amounting to an escalation of brutality—and was it over? With the condo protests continuing? With the Mob possibly involved?

And the girl Lauren, the "lost soul" Margaret had called her, washed up in Susie's house like a wounded dolphin on a beach.

Somewhere in the midst of this progression lay her own act in the Don't Ask, Don't Tell protests. Shortly before she left the commune. Maybe *why* she left—that and the disgust with Greg. The police weren't doing much, a loose bunch around the entrance to the local Defense Department offices, until some demonstrators threatened to occupy the building's first floor. At that point the cops tightened into a line and batons came out. Insults were tossed, as well as rocks and soda cans—she remembered a Pepsi splattering on the steps. It was exciting, electrifying. And at the edge of the plaza where Susie stood, a low, neglected brick border wall had some loose bits of mortar. With the pole of her sign—"Gay Rights Are Human Rights!!!"—she banged at the chinks, hoping to pry out a piece. To her surprise, an entire brick loosened enough for her to yank it away. She moved into the main mass of people and launched it. Scores of people were throwing things now.

She admired the arc as it sailed high over her fellow protesters. What an arm for a small person! She wasn't aiming at anyone in particular, just making sure it cleared the front line of her comrades. She had a clear view when it came down on the face of the young cop, crashing into his left cheek, eye, forehead.... So much like what happened to little Matty!

In the confusion she wasn't identified—no sophisticated video surveillance back then—nor did she ever find out how well the cop recovered. Dozens were arrested, including her, and "several" police were reported "injured," but after a night in jail she and her friends were released without further charges. None of them mentioned the incident to her; perhaps they hadn't seen her throw the brick. Greg had been elsewhere in the crowd.

In the absence of repercussions, the assessment of motive, action, result was left to her alone. That night, when Greg ranted about the "pigface morons" deserving everything they got, she cringed, and ever since then, the face of the wounded cop had wedged in her mind. It became her own wound for more than a quarter century, something she shared with no one as she struggled to reconcile what she'd done with her commitment to respect and dignity for all.

Since then, despite her admiration for anarchist fighters, she'd never hurled so much as a pebble, not even at rallies against the cops' murder of unarmed Blacks. The four times she'd been arrested were all for failing to "disperse" when ordered. But now she'd gotten sucked into a violent mess again, and what would she do about it?

She had no claim to moral superiority here. She'd refused to point the police toward Lauren and Sean—was that smart? Because if Sean went on to commit the arson.... And then she'd kept quiet about Joe's intentions to "take care of it" himself ... could she have stopped him, or at least warned the kids to be careful?

Even with Margaret she couldn't discuss her own culpability, it was too painful.

She couldn't *really* believe that Joe had paid goons to take down Sean— but what *could* she believe? Being such a muddled, complicit person herself, did she have any right to make decisions in these matters? But *not* deciding, *not* acting—as she'd always lectured people—was a type of action.

When she dared look at Malatesta on the refrigerator, the twinkle in his eye seemed ironic—a cruelty that sent her into a profound gloom.

If she didn't know what to do, was she totally useless? Were the principles she'd always revered empty, or was she incapable, at a critical moment, of applying them to real life?

The aging brick-tosser drained one cup of coffee after another, shaken to her core, with too little energy to make a decision or even take herself back to bed. If it were possible to go bankrupt emotionally, she was close.

At last a clatter in the cupboards brought her out of the daze. It was Eric fishing for a cereal bowl and managing to rattle the whole stack.

At this point Susie tried to stand up, only to find the room whirling about her.

* * *

No, she was *not* going to take it easy all day. After the dizzy spell she lay down briefly on the sofa, which smelled a tad funky from Eric's night there; then she popped up again, despite the young people ganging up on her, threatening to take her to the emergency room. "I'm fine!" she snapped. "It's the heat, that's all."

"But it could be delayed symptoms from your concussion," Lauren protested. The girl had materialized from upstairs, kneading her eyes with her wrists. Even with bruised forehead and unbrushed dirty hair, in the same flimsy clothes as yesterday, she looked livelier than Susie felt—an unfair advantage.

"I never had a concussion," Susie argued, "and that was over a month ago. Maybe *you* have a concussion. How does your head feel today?"

"Sore," said Lauren.

"Mom, this is a pattern," Eric pressed. "You've been dizzy too often for weeks now."

"Just a few times during this awful weather," Susie countered. "Eric, why don't you put some pants on? In case you haven't noticed, we have a guest." In his shorts he looked almost as absurd as Joe, which was something she didn't want to think about.

"I want you to see a doctor," her son continued firmly. "If you won't go right away, call and make an appointment."

"That's an excellent idea," Lauren agreed.

"Maybe," Susie granted. "If you stop pestering me. But there's no point in calling on a Sunday, I'd just get the answering service. I'll call tomorrow."

To get away from them, she went up to her room but avoided the bed. Instead she sat on her reading chair and, in that instant, made a choice. After her hour of coffee-fueled cogitation and dejection, her decision came without further thought, which made it seem—for the moment at least—inevitable. She found the card tucked inside her dresser and dialed the mobile number.

"Hello," she said, "it's Susie Alioto." And then she explained that the meeting would have to be on her terms, at the place she specified.

An hour later, muttering "Just a little shopping to do," she slipped out before the young people could stop her.

IV

In William Penn's day, the neighborhood later to be called Fairmount was mere hinterland, not so much as a gleam in a developer's eye. Even now, of all the buildings in that sector, only the neoclassical art museum might have attracted his interest. Unfortunately the distinguished sculptor had not allowed him to rotate his bronze neck, and Penn therefore remained oblivious to the little figure slipping along the wide avenue on a quiet, steaming summer morning. If he'd been able to look, would the great Quaker champion of peace and tolerance have understood her motives?

25

At the small sandwich shop several blocks from her house—mostly a takeout place, not popular for weekend brunches—Susie bought a coffee and muffin at the counter and took them to a table in the deserted back room. It was 10:30, too early for lunch traffic, but already the store's air conditioning was losing its battle against the raging humidity.

Shortly after, she saw her appointed companion enter, scan the little room, then look back over her shoulder. That caution gave Susie an involuntary shiver. What if there were surveillance here? What if a video camera, a recording device—

No, stop this. Susie shook off the paranoia as the newcomer sat opposite, hooking her shoulder bag on the top rail of the chair.

"Like I said, it's Sunday, I'm off duty, I wanta take my kids to the pool." She wore a red T-shirt along with baggy brown shorts, and her high forehead trickled sweat. "This better be important."

"You asked for information. You'll have to judge the importance of it."

"I'm all ears. Is that muffin good?"

"I haven't tasted it. Here, do you want some?"

"No, you paid for it, it's your—"

"I insist. I'm not really a muffin person. I just bought it because I don't believe in using a small business's premises without compensating them in some way."

"You're a weird type of radical."

"I'll take that as a compliment.… Here, I'll put half on a napkin. You get the big half."

"Is that a comment on my weight?"

"No! You don't think I'd—"

"I don't know, I'm trying to figure out what kind of person you are, Ms. Not-a-Muffin-Person."

While their eyes locked together, Detective Tate took a healthy bite of the muffin. Susie hid an uneasy smirk. "Not bad," said Tate. "Moist."

She turned again to look back toward the counter—no other patrons in sight. "It would've been more private at the station."

"I told you I'm *not* going to the station, and this is for you only, not your shoes-on-the-furniture partner."

"Shoes on the—?"

"Never mind. I remember how, at the Black Lives Matter rally, you didn't have that sour look like the other officers. They thought we were supporting cop-killers, but you acted like you respected us, or at least understood the point we were making."

"Maybe because I'm, you know, Black myself?" Tate suggested, wiping a crumb from her mouth.

They smiled at each other, tentatively.

"So … you've thought of something more about the riot."

"No, I didn't say that. And it wasn't a riot."

"Not arguing that point," Tate sighed. "What then?"

Susie took a long breath.

"Yesterday," she began in a low voice, "a young man named Sean was assaulted near 11th and Race. His knees were broken with a baseball bat, and he was taken to Jefferson Hospital."

"Yeah?"

"The crime was reported. Your colleagues have a record of it. But I doubt you have the license number of the car the two attackers drove off in. It was a red Mini with a white top, relatively new, with a Pennsylvania license ending in 1597."

Tate quickly drew a pad and paper from her bag, made a note.

"1-5-9-7," Susie repeated.

"Got it. How do you know this?"

"Uh-uh! You agreed you would take what I gave you, not ask how I know."

"Did I say that?"

"You did."

"All right," Tate grimaced. "Like my kids, they remember all sorts of promises I never made…. And this Sean's surname is …"

"I don't know that, but as I said, the incident was reported. Presumably his full name is on the record."

"And you're sure it was reported because …"

After a beat, watching Susie's expression, Tate added, "O-kayyyy…."

Susie was pondering the murky territory she'd stepped into. Murky and mucky: a swamp.

Another moment passed before Tate said, "Is that it?"

Susie had a mental image of the full scene: Herself hunched over a Formica-topped table, providing confidential leads to a police detective. Perspiration budding on their cheeks, the overhead light too harsh and white. A brown stain in Susie's saucer where her nervous hand had spilled coffee.

It was a picture from another dimension—because Susie Alioto had never, ever been a police informant. Yet this person who couldn't be Susie took another step on the same path.

"I guess there's one more thing.... If you check it out, you may find connections to the protests at the new condos in Point Breeze."

"Point Breeze? You mean where that arson occurred?"

"I wouldn't know about arson," Susie lied.

"No, you wouldn't, I'm sure," mused the detective, giving Susie a look that seemed both skeptical and accepting. "But you're saying this baseball-bat knee-whacking connects with the Point Breeze protests—what sort of 'connect' are we—"

"That's all I have."

"Hmmp," said Tate.

"That's everything I can tell you," Susie repeated, feeling she'd said far too much.

"Huh." Then Tate added, "I see, ma'am," stressing the *ma'am*, tart but not nasty.

The detective scarfed one more tidbit of muffin, gave Susie a hard glance, then a soft nod, and as she rose from the table, reached over and tapped Susie's clammy knuckles with her own damp fingers.

Was that a thank-you? A warning?

Susie had no idea. It was all part of the murk and muck.

26

"Shopping? For what?" Eric challenged Susie when she returned to the house empty-handed.

"A muffin."

"A *what*?"

"I felt a strong yen for a muffin. At the little place on Fairmount Avenue. Blueberry."

"Mother, it's 140 degrees out and you've been falling all over yourself! It's dangerous to go traipsing around the neighborhood when you're faint. When are you calling the doctor?"

"Tomorrow, Eric, like I said, tomorrow. I'm not *faint*. What about you—are you off again today?"

"Yeah. And I don't know about going back there if my boss's uncle is a Mafia don."

"That's exaggerating, I'm sure. And what happened to Lauren?"

"She went to the hospital again. To see what's-his-name."

Susie was relieved not to confront Lauren. She'd just betrayed the girl, or at least violated her express wishes, though probably for her own good—was that actual betrayal? Impossible to decide.

Susie headed upstairs.

"Are you going to rest now?" Eric demanded.

"Rest, yes, I'm going to rest, so *you* can give it a rest, *please*."

In her room, as she unhooked her purse from her arm, she felt a vibration inside. She fished out her cell phone to see that she'd missed a call from Joe—the first one in a week. Just after she'd betrayed him to the cops, or at least given them a link that could trace back to him. Creepy! She refused to listen to the message he'd left.

Dropping the little red phone on her nightstand, she flicked it away like it was too hot to handle. She watched it skid a couple of inches and almost topple to the floor. Such a tiny gadget that held such a scalding problem.

Despite having no intention of resting, she lay on the bed because she couldn't face what she had done—and, worse, what she still had to do. Soon, in the damp and sterile air—she hated the air conditioning, it felt so unnatural—she drifted into a stupor.

Julio came in, looking the same as when he left eight years ago, a slim handsome man with long dark hair and a wiry mustache. He asked what she'd been up to.

—*Me?* she retorted. My life hasn't changed, but what about you? Did you get your biochem doctorate?

—Why should you care? You never wrote or called, he pointed out. You haven't even googled me.

—Of course I care. I loved you very much. I mean, I still love you, and right now I don't know why I didn't … just … go with you.

He gave her an ironic look.

—You said it was "impractical." Your job was here, Eric's schooling was here, your friends, your activism.… You said it had to be a "clean break."

—Is that what I told you?

—Frankly, I think the whispers at school embarrassed you. You didn't like being painted as a cradle robber.

—Hah! Our bed was hardly a cradle! But I knew, as I got older.… I mean, I'd get *old* old long before you would. I was already—

—Are you old old now?

Her mind flitted back to her struggles with postmenopausal symptoms during her years with Julio. How, even at the height of their affair, she'd doubted her attractiveness, her hold on him. How she'd known he'd leave long before *he* knew.

—This dizziness thing, she said.… You know my one brother and sister died early, not much older than I am now.

He shrugged, as if dealing with her mental/emotional state were more than he could manage from his spiritual distance.

When she started to protest this indifference, Julio faded, and she panicked. She'd chased him away again! Squeezing her eyes tight, she tried to call him back, but the huge blank ceiling stared at her implacably. Her breath came in shallow gasps. Her head swam in loops through empty space while it remained, physically, on the pillow.

Then Marty Leffler poked his face in.

That was always the way Marty appeared: poking in, not stepping up and committing. The sight of him revived her.

—Get the fuck away from me.

—Oh babe, feisty as ever!

—Come any closer and I'll rip your scummy little whiskers out hair by hair!

Marty gave her a crooked grin, his mustache sinuous and sneaky. Then he did a perfect, mocking imitation of Julio's shrug. His body faded out, and then his face, but his influence remained, like a sour whiff of spit from his clarinet.

—What a goddamn fool I was!

She'd met Marty only weeks after she'd bought the house in Fairmount, a present to herself for her 43rd birthday. Way, way old enough to know better than to take up with a jazz musician, nine years younger, who still saw life as a series of riffs. If that weren't stupid enough, she'd gotten pregnant and told him she was keeping the child. It was time for a child, she'd decided, with total irrationality. Even crazier, she'd thought she could domesticate the jazzman.

The result: He acted interested, spoke of marriage, and hung around just long enough to induce her to give Eric the surname Leffler.

Since he decamped, she'd never once looked for him, not so much as a quick internet search. She'd entertained herself with thoughts of where she would stick the clarinet if he showed up again. More important, she'd embraced single motherhood. Ideas about equal pay and the links between gender inequality, racism and classism stoked her political life. Yet she'd worried from time to time that subjecting her son to childhood without a father … the effects couldn't be measured, but if he'd had a steady male influence, would he have turned into this aloof, unworldly geek who remembered random four-digit numbers but not his pants?

Naturally she loved Eric the way he was; she had faith he'd do something wonderful in the world of mathematics. Still, if you handed him a football, he wouldn't play catch, he'd tell you about the properties of a prolate spheroid (a term she knew because he had in fact used it).

Would she have wanted a more conventional son? The impossibility of knowing such a thing made her feel even more decrepit. Regrets, a large sticky lump in the heart, could not be sorted into separate strands.

And now, no Julio, no Marty (except this faint aroma of old spit), and her latest attempt at true partnership foundering in the murk and muck of the affair with Lauren and Sean.…

It was too much for a too-too-old anarchist who no longer knew what to believe.

Susie did finally sleep, but when she woke around two in the afternoon she felt the opposite of rested. An on-and-off jangle in her brain alarmed her. Was her mind failing her now? Was this a punishment for—?

She sat up and pressed both hands against her skull, terrified. Once again, the sound ended before she understood it was her phone.

Squinting toward the nightstand, she saw Lauren's number on the screen. She collected herself—that's what it felt like, pressing the pieces of her self back together and transporting them as a unit to her reading chair, where she planted her feet firmly on the floor—and then, with her fingers trembling slightly, she returned the call.

Loud traffic noises in the background, and the girl was cursing.

"What's the matter now?"

"I gave it another chance. After he was so mean to me, but I thought, he's in pain, he's all broke. So I went to the hospital again. But then, then … you know what the douche said to me?"

Susie took a sharp breath.

"I mean, I wasn't saying I'd *do* it, I was just, you know, I showed him the picture on my phone and said how with part of the license number they could maybe track down those goons. I was only thinking out loud but he got, like, *violent*, yelling at me. If I tell the cops *anything* that could tie him to the fire and stuff, he's gonna do worse than bust my knees. He'll cut my …"

The voice broke into furious sobs.

"Lauren?" said Susie.

More sobs. "Lauren, try to calm down and—"

"He'll cut my— You won't *believe* what he said he'd—"

"Don't let him scare you! Come back here, we'll talk about it."

A screech of tires.

"For god sake, don't get run over, Lauren!"

27

It sounded like Lauren had reconsidered telling the police about the license plate. Which gave Susie a partial excuse for what she'd already done, so the conversation with Tate wasn't a full betrayal.

Still, there was the other person. Again, it wasn't an absolute betrayal, because she couldn't guess how successful the police would be. Despite their high-tech surveillance techniques, they preserved their age-old inefficiency, and even if they did track down the occupants of the red Mini, they wouldn't necessarily get to Joe. Or if they did, it'd be difficult to prove unless the goons rolled over on him.

Or there might still be another plausible explanation for the whole thing, though by this point Susie couldn't imagine it.

Whatever ... she'd made her one painful choice, which brought on the next one: to face him. But she *couldn't* face him. The image of his tender white belly made her quake with an impossible mix of desire, softness and repulsion.

Also *anger*. At what he'd done, first of all. But beyond that, she was enraged that such a man, if indeed he was the man he now seemed, had made her want him. She was indignant that she'd be hurt by having to break with him. She was heartbroken in advance, and furious about it.

And yet he'd let a week go by without calling or texting, until earlier today—what kind of lover did that? Shouldn't she tell him off on principle? Except that, as an old old *old* woman, did she have any right to demand attention? Maybe he'd been disappointed by their one night together.... Of course he had younger options; he must.

This mess of feelings, not to mention the gloom that threatened to overwhelm her, made it impossible to control herself enough to talk with him. Yet half an hour after the conversation with Lauren, she dialed her voicemail to hear his message.

"Hi, sweetie!" his voice said. "You're all done with school for the year, right? Wanta go out to celebrate? Give me a call."

The word "sweetie" grated, but given their intimacy, she couldn't really object to a term of endearment. The objections ran far deeper than that.

She deleted the message. She hung up. She studied the phone in her hand. She looked at the afternoon sun welling thickly through her bedroom window, lighting thousands of motes of dust that hovered above the rug—an unwelcome commentary on her housekeeping.

Her forefinger stabbed the phone, emphatically punching out the number.

"Hey, sweetie," he answered. "You got my message? How 'bout I take you for an end-of-school-year dinner? You like Thai, right?"

She inhaled deeply, felt her head wobble. "Right, Joe, the semester's over, my grades are in. I'm not … feeling so great, though. I've had some dizziness. Probably just the heat."

"Yeah, it's brutal. You gotta take care of yourself if you go outside. *Hydrate*, that's what everybody says. I went down to Point Breeze this morning to check on the work and it was already like a million degrees."

She hesitated. "Have you had any more problems … there? Since the fire?"

"Naw, it's too hot for the crazies even, the demonstrators. Or maybe they came to their senses about what's good for the neighborhood."

Susie realized he was lying.

"Affordable, middle-class housing," he went on, "it's—"

"You said," she broke in, "you were going to 'take care of' the trouble somehow."

"Heh," he chuckled. "Heh, maybe…. Let's just say, the arsonist asshole?—I heard he won't be settin' no more fires for a while. Or much else."

Susie shuddered. When the nervous spasm quieted, she asked, "And how is Matty? He went for a checkup?"

"Yeah. Vision's coming back good. What they can't do nothing about yet is the scar. Long term, maybe, plastic surgery. I seen him last night, he's fulla energy but he ain't going back to preschool, too much chance he'll get poked in the eye, so he's gonna stay with the neighborhood lady Rita hired to watch him."

"I'm so glad he's doing well," she stated.

Another pause, and Joe said, "I can tell you're not feelin' good. Maybe we shouldn't go out tonight. You should rest up, you don't sound like your old self."

"Joe," she answered, "you don't really know my old self."

In the contemporary hookup culture, Susie had heard, couples broke up by text message. Or by ghosting, simply not responding, acting like the other didn't exist. Her students talked about that.

Of course she would never do such a thing. Nor would she ever break up by phone, which in her view was almost as bad. Nevertheless, this was a season of doing what she would never do.

"I may not know all about you, but I'm *gettin'* to know you," Joe insisted. "And lovin' it. Susie, it's been a long time since, since I met a woman that's, like, I don't know, so genuine."

He was making this more difficult. That was what men did.

"And you, Joe … I so much appreciate … the time we've had together … but there won't be any more."

"Any more what?"

"More … time together."

"Huh?"

"There's no nice way to put it, but we're too different. Our values, our lifestyles. I can't see you again."

"*What?*"

"I just can't, Joe, I can't be with you anymore."

Such a silly phrase, Susie thought: *be with.* So accurate in some ways, so oblique in others.

While she reflected, she missed a couple of his expostulations. As she tuned back in, he was exclaiming, "I treated you good! The best places! The money I spent on you! And you never told me *shit* about your little anarchist pals. What I found out, I got on my own, no thanks to you. I been straight up with you, but now you give me this, *this* dumbass excuse, *'lifestyle'*—what's that mean anyway? How dare you throw crap like that at me? Why'd I ever bother with you?"

As his rant continued, Susie pushed the disconnect icon on her phone. Then she heaved the phone against the bedroom wall. By the time it landed, it had a big crack in its red case.

All a big joke then? He'd dated her, fucked her, merely in the hope of extracting information? His omelets, the tales about his nonna, meeting his niece—just fakery?

She didn't want to believe it, and in the back of her mind she realized that he'd called for a date *after* getting to Sean, and yet her overwhelming rage said she'd been used, nothing more than that. *Used.*

She staggered to her feet and headed downstairs. Coffee maybe.

On the steps the dizziness hit again. Bewildered, she told herself that, like the great Malatesta with his delicate health, she had to push through any obstacle that tried to stop her. False lovers. Mafia goons. Brainless arsonists. This goddamn vertigo. But how could she push when she felt so weak?

Clasping the handrail, she was startled when the front door suddenly burst open.

It was Lauren, whom she'd given a key.

After Susie looked up at the sound, she couldn't locate her feet on the stairs again—they'd been misplaced. She stumbled. Then she fell, hard. The girl screamed.

28

Freed from all chores. Not a single responsibility. Nothing whatsoever she had to do. They brought her food, water. They washed her, tidied her hair.

It was such a comfort to be liberated from duty, regrets, intentions, implications.

At some point, they said, she needed to get up and walk, but that effort lay in a hazy future. Right now she could sink back under the sheet and gaze at the empty ceiling that somehow mumbled like a TV commercial. One of her roommate's machines beeped, or was that hers? No matter. A bit of chatter could be heard in the hall, irrelevant. The crack in her hip ached, but at a distance.

Her life had been scoured out, it seemed. Scrubbed clean. Like the tumor on her brain, what did they call it? The doctor had explained, though she didn't care. Benign, probably been there for years, growing ever so slowly. Usually not symptomatic, these things, but in a few cases they led to headaches, seizures, changes in vision or memory, or what she'd experienced, dizziness.

No, what she'd experienced was a decay in moral vision. Perhaps starting when she threw that brick, and leading to other confused and confusing choices. But all that had passed like everything else. Scoured away, leaving the brain and soul vacant now.

When visitors came, Eric and Margaret and the girl, she felt comfortable enough to close her eyes and sleep. In her dreams, back in the commune, she stirred and stirred the stock pot and nobody came in for a meal, none of her friends, lovers, acquaintances—a relief because she didn't know what to say to any of them, not Greg or Marty or Julio or Joe or even Papa Dump.

29

Four and a half days, that was the extent of his mother's hospitalization, but Eric spent them in near-constant panic, and when she came home, the situation felt painful and awkward.

Apparently there were no serious after-effects from Susie's meningioma surgery, but the hip she'd cracked in her fall might deteriorate further, and it was agonizing to see her limp around the house with her half-shaved head. Though she'd been given an ugly metal three-toed cane, she refused to use it indoors, steadying herself instead on the furniture. He thought she should've stayed in the hospital longer, but that was the current state of health care, wasn't it?—hack your skull open and then, as soon as you could sit up, wheel you out the door.

As for Lauren, there was no sign of her leaving, perhaps because she was broke and unemployed and laden with student debt and deep in angry self-pity. This was a large part of the awkwardness: with the girl ensconced in his room, Eric no longer had a place in his mother's house, and he was getting an effing crick in his back from the sofa. Also, now that he'd abruptly quit the coffee shop, there were few other places to escape. Like his college friends, his old crowd from high school was dispersing after a short while back in town. He spent some days hanging out in his favorite comics shop downtown, browsing aimlessly and annoying the proprietor.

Another problem was the aura of sadness that permeated the house. It stemmed, he supposed, from the end of both women's relationships, which in his view should have been liberating. Joe was surely a bad actor, and from what Eric could fathom, Sean of the Busted Knees deserved what he'd gotten. Nevertheless, meals passed mostly in silence, and he began to wonder if he should leave early for Seattle.

To find a decent apartment near the university, it made sense to go out there sooner rather than later. He'd tried looking online, but having never lived more than 40 minutes from home, he had little understanding of the neighborhood descriptors offered by websites: "bohemian lifestyle," "eclectic mix," "relaxed feel," "full spectrum of useful and fun stores." What did any of that mean? Where would he fit? To tell the truth, he was anxious that he wouldn't fit anywhere, and this added to his nervousness about facing his hoped-for mentor, the illustrious Nasrin Sassani.

The only way to decide either social or academic questions would be to get there. But what about his determination to "watch over" his mother? Could he leave her now, after such a big health scare? Would she be okay? Though he distrusted doctors, who in his opinion relied too much on fuzzy (nonmathematical) inference, they'd assured everyone that the tumor problem was resolved. Margaret had come over almost every day to lend a hand, and Lauren, too, for as long as she hung around, offered another watcher-overer. The girl's nurse training might be useful in that respect.

Also, the peculiar bond between Lauren and his mother seemed to have strengthened. One day he'd heard Lauren complain, "The total fuckwad— I almost flunked my classes because I took time off to help him. I mean, I believed in the cause, I *worked* for it, but does he care? No, he's just abusive." She snuffled a while and put her head down on the kitchen table, where she and Susie were sitting. "Sorry," she added in a mumble from under her arm, "I don't wanna be a sniveling little bitch."

"You're often bitchy," Susie agreed, as she treated her own wounds with a strong cup of coffee, "and you are indeed sniveling at the moment ..."

"Mom, that's a little harsh," Eric objected from the refrigerator, where he was fetching a snack.

"... but you're not little in body, nor in spirit either. I think I see that much."

"Really?" the girl said. "You believe that?"

Susie sighed, reached over and patted her gently on the knuckles.

It could've been a heartwarming scene, if Eric weren't naturally wary of sentiment. Even for him, it was touching though peculiar.

Now Lauren was spending time with books Susie gave her, like essays by Malatesta, a biography of Voltairine de Cleyre—the same stuff she'd long ago foisted on her son. The poor girl, her brain might be warped forever. But at least in the short term, he felt he could count on Lauren to keep an eye out for dangers.

He was starting to think better of her overall. She'd done some cooking during his mother's hospitalization, and though she had little talent in the kitchen, he appreciated the effort. The other day, too, she'd praised his graphic novel collection and apologized for forcing him to sleep on the sofa. Unfortunately, Sean's dismissal didn't mean that Eric had a chance of sharing a bed with her. She still had his bed all to herself, and what she'd done to deserve that, other than patch his mother's ear and char veggie burgers—

No, he fended off resentment, because he wouldn't add to his mother's problems. The panic he'd felt when she was hospitalized had, in a way, turned his world upside down. He understood now that Susie had suffered a good deal, not just physically but emotionally, though the full nature of the emotional trauma eluded him. For instance, one night before shuffling up to bed,

Susie stopped by the sofa, where he was trying in vain to wrestle himself into a comfortable position. "Eric, honey," she said, "you know, don't you, that I'm sorry you never had a father."

"A father?" he said, incredulous. He almost laughed. "Isn't it a little late for that?"

"Well, yes, and that's why I'm sorry it didn't happen."

He adjusted his tone. "Mom, what are you talking about? I did fine without a father. *We* did fine. I mean, after what I heard from my roommates about their fathers, I was glad I didn't have one!"

In fact, from Susie's fragmented descriptions of Marty Leffler over the years, Eric knew that was the kind of man he never wanted to meet, with or without the clarinet. Why his mother would start brooding about it now …

One night he managed a talk with Margaret, who'd brought lasagna for dinner. After the meal, Lauren sat in the living room watching political talking heads on TV, and Susie, claiming a headache, climbed slowly to her bedroom. He and Aunt M had some time to themselves as they cleaned up in the kitchen.

"Not good," Eric scowled across the sink, referring to Susie's headache. "Do you think it's—"

"Related to the surgery? Yeah, maybe. She did have her head sliced open."

"What if this goes on? You know, I have to—I mean, my program starts in September, and if I delay too long in finding an apartment …"

"I think you can go whenever you need to."

"Really? It's just that—"

What he couldn't explain, or even formulate to himself, was that in the past days, without a room or bed, without a job, with a slightly intimidating future looming before him, he'd come to cherish his mother's company more than since he was a young child. Minutes with her seemed suddenly precious, and when she hobbled upstairs after dinner, he missed her.

"I'll be here, Eric, checking in every day. Wrap the leftover lasagna, will you? You guys can have it tomorrow."

"But if she has a seizure or something, or falls again …"

"I hope not, but if that happens, Lauren can help."

"Her? … I guess … but," he stepped closer to whisper, "she's not much use at cooking, you know. She burns stuff."

"Well, she's a *project*," Margaret grinned, sliding rinsed plates into the dishwasher. "She gives your mom a mission."

"Huh?"

"Well, you're a finished product, for better or worse—worse, I think.

Why are you using half the box of waxed paper?"

"It won't stay on otherwise! Why doesn't she buy plastic wrap like everyone else? I mean, who says we have to be the ones to save the Earth from plastic?"

Margaret sighed.

"What she needs," Eric grumbled, "is to get her health back. And her life."

"Right," Margaret agreed. "That's what I'm saying."

30

Once the lovely vacancy she'd felt in the hospital dissipated, Susie's head began to rage again. The little old lady in the mirror looked worse than ever, and she knew her lover would have dumped her if she hadn't dumped him first. As for her life of the mind, what of that was left?

Years ago, Eric had called her a "bourgeois anarchist," a phrase he thought was funny. Susie had been furious at the time. One had to live in the world as it was, and in a bourgeois society, one couldn't help but reach accommodations; yet as long as one held firmly to principles—

But how clear was she about those principles now? And if she had no firm underpinning, what point was there in going on? Could she keep teaching? Demonstrating?

So many conflicts kicked up dust in her brain. Whom she'd betrayed, whom she hadn't. Whether she was a collaborator or a responsible citizen. Whether she'd been romanced or simply abused. All this, exacerbated by the sharp stabs from her hip and the aching wound in her scalp, seemed impossible to fit together coherently. When Malatesta's poster reminded her that "Impossibility never prevented anything from happening," she shot back, "What the hell does that *mean* anyway?"

And there was this airheaded, needy girl hanging around, demanding attention. Susie had pushed some books at her, fundamentals of anarchist literature, in the hope of supplying a small measure of education. But since Susie's own relationship to these classics felt troubled, she didn't know what good they might do.

One day when Eric had gone out for a jog—a new commitment to fitness, he claimed, but probably just an excuse to leave the house—Lauren acted sulkier than usual. With no summer classes or job, the girl seemed entirely at loose ends. Over a lunch of tuna sandwiches, which Susie made herself because the girl acted confused about the role of mayonnaise, Susie asked what was wrong.

"Nothing. Nothing. The fucktard called me, that's all."

"That would be Sean," Susie confirmed. "And?"

"Sounding like he thinks we're still together. Like I'll come to the rehab hospital and help him do exercises or whatever. Fuck that."

Susie drew a deep breath and pointed out the obvious. "Well, if you don't want to hear from him, you can stop taking his calls. That's called ghosting, isn't it?"

Susie hadn't needed to apply the technique to Joe because he'd never called again, or emailed, or texted. A clean break.

"Yeah," Lauren said. "It's just"—she paused, staring at her sandwich as if she'd never seen one before—"I was, I mean I thought I was—we were—in it for the whole ride. Long-term. You're not supposed to make assumptions like that, people need to be free to evolve, but I was a *stupid* little sucker."

"It hurts," Susie sighed. "No matter what you tell yourself before or after, it'll hurt for a while. Maybe a long while. But you get over it. Actually, that's wrong. You don't get *over* it, but you go *past* it."

"You're so comforting," Lauren sneered, taking a huge chomp of her sandwich.

"Don't mock me, young lady," Susie barked. "I've *been* there."

With her mouth stuffed, Lauren's eyes widened as if she were surprised that Susie took offense at her rudeness. "Sorry," she mumbled through the food.

"I suppose it's good," Susie went on, "whatever we think of Sean, that he's progressed as far as exercises. When will he be out and about again?"

Lauren gave an exaggerated shrug as she swallowed. "I think he's happy to be holed up in rehab. 'Cause he's scared. The cops called him, said they found the dudes that assaulted him, they want him to ID them. He figures if they're Mob guys, that'll just put him on a worse hit list."

"Huh." To Susie, this seemed too minor an affair for the Mob at large to worry about, but who could predict? She was pleased, at least, that Detective Tate, or others informed by Tate, had nabbed the two thugs, even if nothing more would come of it. That meant her betrayal of principle hadn't been entirely in vain.

"And he was accusing me again. I mean, at the same time he's practically begging me to come be with him, he *insinuates* I showed the cops my license-plate picture. 'Cause if they get anything out of the goons, the cops could dig in deeper, that's what he thinks."

The girl gave Susie a wary glance, then pretended to be absorbed in picking a blob of tuna off her T-shirt.

"They could find out who hired the goons," Susie said.

"Yuh." Lauren licked the tuna off her forefinger, then mumbled, "Your brunch pal."

"And *why* they were hired."

Lauren acted as if she hadn't heard.

"Could *you* identify them?" Susie asked.

The girl shook her head violently.

"Look," Susie challenged her, "let's come clean. You weren't directly involved in the arson, were you?"

"Me? No way!"

The girl's mayonnaise-smeared expression of astonished innocence seemed only slightly fake, and Susie went on.

"Or that other mysterious guy in your little cell—Maxie?"

More astonishment.

"Okay, I believe you weren't part of it."

Another decision loomed ahead, and Susie took it. "And so I'll tell you that I informed the police about the car and the license plate—the entire number that Eric remembered. Because I think the thugs that beat up Sean should be charged. And if Joe Sambucco, the condo developer who is no longer my friend, hired them, I don't mind if the police arrest him too. And if Sean set the fire, I don't care if it gets traced back to him. In fact, if he's guilty, I hope it does."

There! Susie had laid it all out. With some bitterness, but also relief.

Lauren became deeply involved in managing the sandwich, from which she'd eaten the middle, leaving two floppy ends. She wouldn't look at Susie. After a while, though, she sighed and let her hands drop to her lap.

"For your information," she mumbled, "Maxie's female. And I think she and Sean— Never mind."

* * *

After Susie's confession, she thought Lauren might leave. But the girl didn't. She stayed on, and Susie was halfway glad to have her, a distraction if nothing more. Susie's spirits lifted a bit.

She also had a talk with the hero himself, Malatesta, about whether she should be labeled a traitor to the creed for talking to cops and implicating a would-be revolutionary.

She approached Errico defiantly, face to face, where his head floated on its stark background of red and black. She had always, she reminded him, charted her own way, especially since the brick incident, and she didn't need approval from anyone.

"I'm not making excuses," she asserted. "I acted according to conscience. You always had your reasons, I have mine. Even if they're hard to explain."

The idealist on the refrigerator replied with his ever-twinkly eyes, his ever-ambiguous hint of a smile.

31

For dinner on July 3, Margaret brought a roast chicken, and conversation around the table turned to the demonstration the next day in which TeachPeace would participate.

"The idea is," said Margaret, "to celebrate Independence Day by recognizing that America's a nation of immigrants who came here in search of freedom. We'll support those who are coming here now, the refugees, the undocumented. *Their* right to independence from fear and government persecution. We're gathering near Independence Hall."

"You're going?" asked Susie.

"Yeah, I'm planning to."

"Then I'll meet you there."

"Whoa, whoa!" said Eric. "Mom, you can't do that."

"Who says?"

"You're in no shape to be out on the street!" He gestured emphatically with a drumstick, determined to stop this craziness. "Besides, last time you got hurt!"

"This time," Susie countered with a sidelong look at Lauren, "we shouldn't have any black-suited window-busters."

"He's right," said Margaret. "This is too soon for you, Susie. Wait till the fall, cooler weather, till you have time to—"

"I've had plenty of time to," Susie mocked.

"You're barely a week out of the hospital!" Eric snapped.

"But … you know, I can go with her," piped Lauren.

Astonished, Eric stared from his mother, with her half-bald scalp and bandaged incision, to the girl whose goon-bruised forehead had healed only as far as a mottled yellow. He pictured them in the street, the dim-brained leading the surgically-repaired-brained.

"It's not a march this time, right, Margaret? Just a rally in one place," Susie insisted. "I'll take it easy. I have my cane. I'll wear a scarf to keep the sun off my head."

"You haven't been using the cane enough," Lauren chided.

"I use it when I *need* it."

"If you're so determined," Margaret mulled, "I'll come here to pick you up. We'll all stick together, and if it's too crowded or hot, we'll find a place to sit, duck into a restaurant or something."

"Don't give in to her!" Eric yelped, but he felt helpless to clamp down. He'd booked a cheap overnight flight to Seattle next week, so whatever temporary rationality he might impose today would vanish with him.

There was no stopping these nuts, he mused. He'd be out there meeting with the formidable Nasrin in her spartan, book-lined office, or sitting in a coffee shop working up the nerve to speak to strange women, or lying on his bed in a lonely, underfurnished apartment, and they'd be here at this table, planning risky, useless acts on behalf of people they didn't know and wouldn't ever meet. Only a wild-eyed anarchist, like the one staring at his back from the refrigerator, could appreciate this lack of common sense.

"What about you?" Margaret was saying.

Angrily Eric ripped a slice of meat from the drumstick before he realized she was talking to him.

"Me?"

"Yeah, why don't you come if you're so worried about your mother?"

He gulped down the chicken, looking from one woman to another, from a friendly challenge (Margaret) to a quizzical frown (Lauren) to a studiously noncommittal expression (Susie).

"You people are totally, *totally*—" He searched for a word strong enough. There wasn't one.

"I suppose," he said at last, "somebody should be there to haul you all to the hospital. Or bail you out of jail."

"I don't think either will be—" Margaret started to answer, but he interrupted her.

"All *right*," he coughed. "One time. I'll go rally with you *one* time.... Remind me," he added just to be obnoxious, "what are we protesting again?"

His heart jumped when his mother smiled.

Acknowledgments

The principal characters of this book have been with me for years, through multiple attempts to find the right story for them. Their development owes an immeasurable amount to my fellow members of the Working Writers Group in Philadelphia, notably Ann de Forest, Louis Greenstein, Mark Lyons, Vikram Paralkar, Nathaniel Popkin, David Sanders, Debra Leigh Scott and Miriam Seidel.

I'm grateful as well to the entire staff of Finishing Line Press that brought this book into print, especially Christen Kincaid, Elizabeth Maines McCleavy, Leah Huete de Maines, and Jackie Steelman.

As always I thank my wife, Peggy Gordon, for putting up with me and easing me through frequent ridiculous crises. When the revolution finally arrives, folks like Ms. Gordon and Ms. Alioto will rule.

After being born in Pittsburgh, **Sam Gridley** lived in Camden, Providence, Bristol, Westchester, Inglewood, Palos Verdes Estates, Torrance, Redondo Beach, Northridge, Culver City, Berkeley, Oakland, Cambridge, Brighton, London, Palo Alto, Bellefonte, Baltimore, Lyndhurst, Rutherford, and perhaps other communities he has forgotten. This was before the age of 29. Since then he has settled in Philadelphia and scarcely budged.

As an author, he has published two novels, *The Shame of What We Are* and *The Big Happiness*, as well as stories and satire in more than sixty magazines and anthologies. He has received two fellowships from the Pennsylvania Council on the Arts and a Wallace Stegner Fellowship from Stanford University.

Married for many years, Sam has two grown children, one neurotic dog and a small backyard where several gerbils are buried. He hangs out at the website Gridleyville.blog.

CPSIA information can be obtained
at www.ICGtesting.com
Printed in the USA
LVHW040356220721
693237LV00002B/172

9 781646 625444